Sophia

Also by Michael Bible

NOVELLAS

Cowboy Maloney's Electric City

Simple Machines

CHAPBOOKS

My Second Best Bear Rug

Gorilla Math

Sophia

A NOVEL BY

MICHAEL BIBLE

MELVILLE HOUSE
BROOKLYN · LONDON

SOPHIA

First Melville House printing: December 2015

Melville House Publishing   8 Blackstock Mews
46 John Street   and   Islington
Brooklyn, NY 11201   London M4 2BT

mhpbooks.com   facebook.com/mhpbooks   @melvillehouse

Library of Congress Cataloging-in-Publication Data
Bible, Michael.
  Sophia : a novel / Michael Bible.
    pages ; cm
  ISBN 978-1-61219-472-1 (pbk.)
  ISBN 978-1-61219-473-8 (ebook)
  I. Title.
PS3602.I24S67 2015
813'.6—dc23
                                        2015019003

Designed by Adly Elewa

Printed in the United States of America
10 9 8 7 6 5 4 3 2 1

I dreamed a knife like a song you can't whistle.

—Frank Stanford

Sophia

1

I'm a nautical man on my small filthy yacht since the bank took my house. I should cruise around the blue world gazing at the jumping fish but I've become transfixed by a praying mantis praying on a piece of toast. The Holy Ghost touches my shoulder to say hello.

Not now, I say. This mantis is praying his prayer.

I'm a holy fool on the hunt for something worthy. I chase the saints of all religions and long to join their team. They call me the Right Reverend Alvis T. Maloney but things are becoming unstable in the Goldilocks zone. Dusk is a bonfire of wild sunflowers and across the night an archer aims his bow. That which has been is that which shall be. It's Sunday morning in America. Twenty-first century. Year of the Dragon.

Eli, Eli. You are my last friend. You live with your brother Boom on the edge of town. You know the day of the week everyone was born on, a calendar savant in suspenders and a black trucker hat. Eyes like blue marbles, a Marlboro dangles from your lip. Your father tried to beat smarts into you and that pedophile baptized you in the Mississippi River. Be my Sancho, Eli, my man Friday, my Robin, my Dr. Spock drunk on the job. Your hat says, Easy come, easy go. I light your smoke.

Everything is always better ten years ago. They say we were once the great Southern Bohemia, now it's people eating shrimp cocktail and complaining about the AC in the juke joint. Eli, you've fallen for a teenage electric fiddle player on stage playing "Hard Day's Night."

John Lennon was born on a Thursday, you say. John Lennon was a good man.

I take my meals at the Starlight Diner in town, a greasy spoon near the harbor where I keep my boat. In a back booth a woman calls her lover Daddy. A drunk fat man cries with his drunk fat son. I'm waiting for the narcotics to rush in. I'm waiting to regain the good heat. Eli, you've soiled yourself in the bathroom due to an excess of cocaine and Budweiser. Your suspenders are falling off. There are a thousand more jobs at the bullet factory. Alabama is beating LSU.

I'm the lazy priest of this town's worst church, nearly defrocked for lascivious behavior with female parishioners. I want to die for the King of Kings but can't quite get it right. I long to lounge with Him in that upper room but I'm losing the desire. I council Tuesday, who I'm in love with, when her mind goes wrong. She wears a single dreadlock in her hair. In the confessional I undo my clerical collar and fire up a spliff.

My fantasy is to commit suicide on the moon, she says. I would open my helmet and explode.

I see, I say puffing smoke.

My daddy was like Jesus. A carpenter and a Jew, dead at thirty-three. Except my daddy had a Tasmanian devil tattoo and a drinking problem.

Interesting, I say.

Puff puff.

Go on.

Jesus was the first Christian saint. A martyr for the cause of himself. He was crucified, dead, and buried. The third day he rose from the dead to sit at the right hand of God the Father Almighty. He spoke in nonsense stories on earth—mustard seed, camel through the eye, buried talents. Wept in the garden like a wuss. He is Man and God and Word. Logos and Agape. Selah. He died, but he really didn't. Amen?

Big blue awful day out there. A woman in a burqa texts outside the open chapel window, a little boy shoots her with a water gun.

At the end we're all just numbers, you say, Eli. Height, weight, credit score, IQ, social.

Very simple machines, I say. But things can be so complex. For example, could Tuesday and I just take it to the bathtub? Get wet and see what happens?

The cotton is coming in huge bricks on flatbed trucks and the clouds are God's hobby sculptures—a heart, a lion, a gun. The man on the phone keeps yelling, Stop talking, stop talking, stop talking! There's a new girl working at the Starlight. Skin of an Aztec, long hair falling down her back like a braid of black smoke. Her eyes are sapphire. She keeps returning my gaze.

Get me another gimlet, Eli. Make it a double. My shoe's got holes and a mailman's pounding on my door. The letter says the farm's been sold and my uncle's gone to heaven. Last of my family. You've got rib sauce all over your face, looks like blood. Like you've been shot.

Church picnic. Tuesday says she's Joan of Arc. Her sword is silver.
I am the Maid of Orleans, she says.
Get off the roof, I say. The sausages are burning.
I am rubbing God's beard between my thighs.
If you don't get down, I will burn you at the stake.

Behind the abandoned hospital on a peach tree hangs one rotten peach. Two black wizards approach dumpsters behind the church, black hoods and staffs. They are cosplay people maybe worshiping a comic book. They cast spells on each other, high five, chest bump. They pretend the peach is forbidden fruit. They wear jester's shoes and speak Elizabethan. They try to light the Sunday sports section on fire with their eyes.

The Ole Miss Rebels botch the winning field goal on homecoming. Yellow leaves are falling and that's all I have to say about that.

Eli, you are one of my flock, but now we drink gimlets and eat painkillers on the square. Your father looked like Uncle Jesse from *The Dukes of Hazzard*. Your mother looked like that lady from *Hee Haw*. Your sister was a friend of mine back in high school. Me and Boom were drinking buddies in the late nineties. But now is now and then was then. The flag is always at half-mast.

St. James kneels and asks forgiveness and is stoned to death. Doves scatter as the rocks crack his bones. Their wings make the sound of gloved hands clapping. As a child he loved to fish at night. Alone with the stars and surf.

I like Elvis in Memphis, late period. Karate Elvis. Fat Elvis going through the drive-thru on his motorcycle. Letting the black girls touch his belt buckle after the show. TLC. Hawaii come back. The Jordanaires. The smell of the Jungle Room fills me—Quaaludes and sweat. Kung fu in the mornings and the evenings dying in the john.

Last century they drilled holes in heads. They gave the shock treatment to rid the voices. I tried to cure with gentle sermons. Things are different now. For instance, I robbed a blind man at a rest stop on the way to New Orleans. Then later a woman with her jaw wired shut on the streetcar hummed "Hey Jude."

Eli, it has come to my attention that Tuesday is sleeping with the owner of the army/navy surplus store. An ex-quartermaster in the merchant marines. Goes by White Mike Johnny. He wears an eight ball pinky ring and cell phone holster. Tuesday is reading Soldier of Fortune magazine in her kitchen. Painting her toenails camo.

Talk to me, I say. What does he got that I ain't got?
He allows me to fire automatic weapons on the weekends.
But I will perform constant cunnilingus.
He has a ski boat.
I play the piano in the dark.
That's another reason I don't love you.

St. Peter is crucified with his head down and his feet up. I'm unworthy to be crucified in the same form and manner as the Lord, he says. Over the crowd he can see a woman in the marketplace. The wind has blown up her robe and he can see her bare white bottom and the trees are moving in the distance. Olive trees dying in the shade.

•

Boom is in the hospital again. Eli, you call him and hand me the phone.

Boom, I say.

I'm in pain, he says. Some pain.

I'm sorry.

Sometimes I have pain. And then sometimes I don't.

OK, I say.

OK, he says.

I've seen to the sick and studied sin. I've sailed my boat around the Cape of Good Hope. I've fly-fished in Chile dropped from a helicopter. I've played nine holes before lunch. I know the right way to drive a sports car, when to fold 'em. But now life is just people with their eyes begging for answers I don't have. Each day seems an easier one to let go, but still on and on. The lights never go off at the neighbor's and there is never anything good to eat on this boat.

Here's the problem with modern medicine, Eli. It keeps you alive longer but it's not pretty.

Tuesday is in the river washing her hair. White Mike Johnny drowned last week and she mourns him. Clemson beat Auburn. A man dances on the roof of his Honda in the church parking lot, chugging Cutty Sark, blasting The Rush Limbaugh Show. The creek looks weird and fluorescent. The neighbor girls play Lewis and Clark, molest a male Sacajawea. Then a peach sunset.

Let's talk about this country's problem with love. Let's talk about the silver-haired blowhards on the street making deals, getting ahead at the office. Best case you end up on a feeding tube watching reruns of *Jeopardy*.

    I thought you were the shepherd, you say, Eli.

    Yes, but they are still the lambs.

    I'm a lion.

    No, you're not.

    Well, I damn well fucking am.

    What were we talking about before *Jeopardy*?

    Love?

I've formed a little band called Roy G. Biv. It's a noise band kind of thing with a man who just stands nude, a girl on trombone with unshaven legs, and a man with a bullhorn named Finger. We are on the bandstand at the bar after a bluegrass act and there are shouts of hate and we love the hate. The main purpose of the band is to be despised.

Tuesday's broken me. I'm out here on the poop deck looking at blue blank sky. I can't find a bright side to this. I call her.

    We could've done some things, I say.

    Like what?

    Walked out of restaurants together, not paid the bill.

That's love to you?
It's a kind of love, yes.

I've sailed to New York in my mind. Nice to be out on the water and look out at the old Lady Liberty and the new phallic Freedom Tower, a sweet erection up to heaven.

St. Blanchard is caught between the river and the road then dragged back to town by all the women whose hearts he'd broken. They tie him to a raft, pile yellow roses, and light them on fire. They love him but want him to never break another heart.

A fugitive walks through the football stadium filling with snow. A trillion stars flicker in the theoretical multiverse. Eli, I wonder if Jesus ever had a wet dream?

A fat kid brought a sword to the snowball fight. I walk around all day with my sweater on backward. The Holy Ghost creeps in the shadows of my house. I am under my bed and she opens my drawers. A Chinese woman named Nono at the snowball fight wants to ask you something, Eli. She wants to know your name.

Eli, you say.
I'm Nono, she says.
You stare into her eyes.
I want to play chess today, you say.

I'll play, says Nono.

Strip chess, says Eli.

Set up the board, she says. Your move.

I have a dream about Tuesday wearing nothing but a magician's hat.

Come love me, she says. Abracadabra.

We can die out here of hypothermia, I say.

You never want to do anything where you might die, she says.

In the hospital Boom wears a fake mustache with his chemo bald head. There is a fire at the travel agency and the acrobat with HIV is doing somersaults in the graveyard. I feel like Charlie Chaplin I'm so weak in the knees. I am fading in and out of sleep. Thanksgiving was a bust.

There is bliss out there somewhere. Take this, the waitress with the sapphire eyes from the Starlight has entered the confessional. I light a spliff and we chat.

A bear dream visits sometimes, she says.

What is the bear doing?

Catching salmon in the river.

Are you the salmon or the bear in the dream?

I am the river.

•

Eating is the worst thing you can do to your teeth. Living is the worst thing you can do to your body. The best thing for your health is to never have been born.

I only love the ugly pretty girls. Too much beauty makes me sick. If a woman has no scars she doesn't interest me. The greater the flaw, the greater the beauty. I grab a stool and listen to the old men place their orders at the Starlight. One can't eat wheat and the other wants his toast dry. A woman in an eye patch screams for Albert but no one looks up. Maybe there is no one named Albert or maybe Albert is tired of answering her. The girl with the sapphire eyes takes my order. Cup of coffee, black. Two eggs, scrambled. She's in a short dress, blue, intellectual. Her father owns the place. She steals philosophy from the bookstore and devours men. Her real name is Honeysuckle, but everyone calls her Darling.

2

Eli, everywhere I go, dirty looks. These people that pray in restaurants before their meals. These people with their ideas about ideas. Asking me for forgiveness? And what are these people's great sins? Men forget to put the toilet seat down. Women use up all the hot water. All domestic hell breaks loose and they're pounding my door. Keep a clean heart, I tell them. Whatever that means.

Failure is the most interesting trait. Like the story of the serpent and the two orchard thieves. Sometimes you're like Texas, Eli, one vast contradiction. Sometimes you're like nothing at all. In the confessional Tuesday says I am emotionally crippled. How can the lamb diagnose the shepherd? These days this preacher could use a nurse. A morphine drip and a kind bedside manner.

The big moon, Eli. The supermoon. The one you've talked about for so long. Only happens once every four hundred years and now it's cloudy. Boom calls and says he's half in heaven and Christ has sky-blue eyes. He says heaven is 72 degrees and has really good Italian food. Let's head to the bar with the dueling pianos, Eli. Let someone sing that awful, beautiful song by Billy Joel and weep. I feel I could rob a Dairy Queen right now, but I'm too drunk to drive.

Boom will never go fishing on a lake again. He is close to death but cannot die. He has been dying for fifteen years. I was asked to give him ease in his final months but he just keeps on dying.

Seize the day, Eli. Break a leg. Put the pedal to the metal where the rubber meets the road. Pull my chain. Pull a fast one. Pull the wool over my eyes. Put a cork in it. Buy the farm. Bite the dust. Eat my dust. Kick the bucket. Sharp as a tack. Stiff as a board. Sweating blood. Sweating bullets. Happy as a clam. Raining cats and dogs. Buckle up. Buckle down. Play with fire. Go with the flow. Easy come, Eli, easy go.

Things are so bad and then I remember the secular saints: Beethoven, van Gogh, the drummer from Def Leppard.

I am trying to keep to the root of things. There's spit on the corners of my mouth. I'm reciting Lucky's speech from *Waiting for Godot*.

It's OK that you're going mad, you say, Eli. But can you stop doing it so close to me?

Sports of all sorts, I say. All kinds of dying flying sports.

St. Simon is killed with a saw. At his wedding Jesus turned water into wine. His screams are heard a mile away.

Eli, I find you drunk and stumbling near the fire station.

I can't make the parade tonight, you say.

The parade was yesterday.

Either way I can't make it.

Tuesday has run away with a jam band called The String Cheese Incident. She is selling something named heady goo balls in the parking lot. She loves a man named Marlin, a roadie.

I'm in the high mountains, she says, where earth meets sky.

Do you remember the restaurant we used to go to? The one with the stuffed polar bear?

What about it?

It blew up.

The white roses outside the lady chapel are wilting from too much rain. Boom calls and says he has a good view of a robin nesting outside his window. He watches the mother vomit food into the baby's mouth. Sometimes Boom says he can only smell. On his worst days, he says, olfactory is all he's got. Then his senses will come rushing back strangely. I can feed him a peppermint and he can hear again. I can play him Beethoven and his skin will tingle. But the sound of a sneeze can put him in a coma for days. A full episode of *Wheel of Fortune* is a miracle. He is hoping in the spring he will see a baby robin fly.

Eli, let's spend the better part of the afternoon drinking gin and playing chess. Two lost gentlemen seeking the daily fluff. We are on your back porch overlooking the cotton when two Canadians land a balloon in the field. They have champagne. We toast that they are still alive after their rough landing. We toast that you are Eli and I am Maloney. We toast that everyone alive is still alive.

St. Sebastian is tied to a tree and archers shoot him full of arrows. He is buried, rises from the dead, heals a woman. Then is beaten to death by an emperor and left in a ditch.

Pretty good story if it were true, you say, Eli.

There's no truth anymore, I say. The truth died in 1865.

Darling pours me black coffee at the Starlight. She thinks I should spend more time on the water. That is where I am happy.

Have you ever been to Greenwich Village, she says. That's where all the poets lived.

Once. Long ago, I say. Before the Lord got me.

•

Eli, I want to sail around the horns and never quite arrive at a final destination. We can visit islands so remote they don't have names. Live among natives. Yet as we age the possibilities grow less endless. The windows of opportunity don't slam, they shut quietly in the dark. We're always another cup of coffee away from the end. I'll be damned if my adventures are spent sitting in this boat. We are out floating in space, the earth our ship. Riding round the big star. There is too much chattering about the end and not enough shutting up about the now. Out on the sea, Eli, me and you and the ones we love. We could leave the harbor with a little push.

Eli, we snort heroin and go to the bookstore. You ask for art books. I want abstract art, you say. I only like art that is abstract. I give you a book. Is this art, you ask. I don't know, I say. This is fantastic, you say. This is fantastic! I show you another book and you ask, Is *this* art? And I say, I don't know. And you say, This is fantastic! The girl at the counter (the one with nice breasts) says, You might like Dalí. Dalí was a pornographer, you say and throw the book in her face. On the ride home you say sometimes I remind you of a panther.

Tuesday overdosed during the fifth encore of the Red Rocks show. I pick her up at the airport and she looks clear after her hospital stay. The wizards are at the back of the cotton field throwing the football. The Rebels lose to Bama.

•

Eli, can you clear the hospital room? Boom and I need to speak.

What do you want done in your absence, I ask him.

I want you to take my saddle off the wall and strap my bones to my pony and set her free, Boom says.

OK.

I was happy in my life, he says, there was a lot of pain but I enjoyed that, too.

I know, I say.

There are reports of Satan in the physical world, Eli. A cub scout saw eerie boot prints near the roller skating rink.

Was there a smell of patchouli and blood, I ask the scout.

It was exactly that odor, sir.

Never cross your heart and hope to die, I say. Always step on a crack. You can never break your mother's back.

I carry this here pink foot of a rabbit for luck and good graces, he says.

I give him fifty bucks and send him on his way.

Eli, Nono found your bike in a ditch.

She's a very sexy woman, you say.

She's sixty-five years old, I say.

She's an artist, you say.

Are you sleeping with her?

Maybe I am and maybe I am.

•

St. Juan is scourged and pressed to death with weights. His brothers, Felix and Philip, are beheaded. Their mother, too, with the same sword.

Boom dies on a Friday, like Christ. We send him off in the following way: I hire the Confederate drummer boy from the local Civil War reenactors group, he plays light taps throughout. I give a reading from the Holy Bible. Valley of the shadow, etc. We strap Boom to the pony. I give the Eucharist. Weed brownies as the body, moonshine as the blood. I shoot a pearl-handled pistol in the air. Eli, you slap the pony and it runs toward the moon.

3

The fair comes to town with its psychedelic lights and expensive corn dogs. Dick Dickerson, the mayor, is a bald man who owns a pawnshop. He's a loudmouth in love with Tuesday. A prideful atheist, he hands out the ribbons in the ugly dog contest. We ride the Ferris wheel up to the highest point and drink from the whiskey pint and the whole town smiles below us.

The sun is pouring down those sweet UV rays. Tuesday is leaving for Bangkok tomorrow. We go to a bar. She bends over in tight jeans to put a quarter in the jukebox.

She's a keeper, says the bartender.

She's so much better than me, I say.

They all are, he says. Trick is never let 'em know it.

We visit Boom's grave.

Why are you wearing two watches, Eli?

This one is on our time, this one is on Hollywood time.

You didn't really answer the question.

●

In Rome thirty-nine saints are forced into a freezing lake but after three days they still show signs of life. Unable to be killed by freezing, they are burned, their ashes thrown into the air.

What's the point of these saint stories, you say, Eli.

I'm trying to find a way to die with honor.

How 'bout trying to live with honor?

One thing at a time, I say. One thing at a time.

Tuesday calls from Thailand.

There are many wild dogs, she says.

Have you found any truth?

I have orgasms when I touch my belly button.

When are you coming home?

I have no home.

I thought you might say that.

The man at the pharmacy wears a ponytail and a Ghostbusters T-shirt. We get Xanax for the fear and Oxy for the existential pain and some gin to add a bit of flash. Then to the Starlight with the pink flamingo wallpaper for BLTs, then to the harbor. Eli, with Boom gone you sleep on my boat.

How does it all end, Maloney?

Good night, Eli. I have no answers.

Eli, we must go to the south side of town to find my missing bandmate, Finger. The people in this filthy squat wear flea collars, it's that bad. Finger is freegan, which means he doesn't care for money. He rides comically large bikes and has a homemade sailboat tattoo over his heart. I find him on the floor, flies on his face. We take him to the boat.

Don't you have anywhere to go, I ask.

Somewhere maybe, he says, someplace.

I give Finger some heat from my bottle of gin.

My mother died in a city by the mountains, he says. I never wanted to sleep under a roof.

The Holy Ghost visits my sleep. She tells me a story. It is a story about gold bricks and blow jobs. I wake up drunk at the Starlight.

You were talking in your sleep, says Darling.

An angel in the wild, I say.

You're high.

Will you come to my boat?

No, she says.

I'm sorry, I say. A very sorry saint.

Eli, let's ride your new motorbike and sidecar out to the countryside. There are foggy pastures where we cruise. A barefoot man rides a horse bareback. A teenager does a doughnut on a four-wheeler. Whole fields of white cotton grow. We go to Wise Jane's. A former Delta debutante turned intellectual redneck. She once slow danced with Matthew Barney and he gave her a piece of the Berlin Wall. We take golf carts to the lunar surface, a patch of sand in the middle of the cotton field. We howl at the moon and say wild toasts and confess sins. Eli, you are screaming at the huge moon like a banshee.

St. Lucy's eyes are gouged out. But she regains her sight. Then is beheaded.

When do they get saint status, you say, Eli.

I don't remember, I say. Pass the wine.

I've been putting tiny ships into bottles. You cannot know the ancient secret of the ship bottlers. Don't touch. View it on the mantle as the mystery it is. Out the window the carnival truck leaves town. We eat astronaut ice cream from the children's museum.

You're a son of a bitch, Maloney.

What's that you say?

You heard me.

Lord, you give us tornadoes and purple sunrises. We praise your beautifully illogical ways. You performed great miracles long ago and nothing since. Why such confusion? We love you, wonderful idiotic Lord.

Eli, I counsel a woman who resembles Sigourney Weaver in the movie *Aliens*. I'm drunk at the session.

Are you saying your prayers at night, I ask.

My mother told me I should quit the prayers and do yoga, she says.

Yoga, I burp. There should be a jihad on yoga.

Finger gets a job at the pawnshop. One night he is sitting behind the counter reading *Lolita* and Dick Dickerson comes in and slaps him with his antique cane.

No reading, says Dick Dickerson.

OK, says Finger.

Then Dick throws the book at the wall.

Become a better person on your own time, he says.

Eli, we find a note Boom wrote you when you were young:

There are not many true sunflowers and you are one of them. You are a small bird with small wings. For you there is music that no one else can hear. Yes, you are a bird with tiny, tiny wings. You follow the sun like a soul reaching to heaven. There is music that only you can hear. You are Eli.

Today I'm viciously attacked by BB gun fire. Is there a sniper in the trees? Then an all-out ambush of twelve-year-olds. I run back onto the boat.

Finger, thank God you're here. I'm being attacked.

You must have crossed them, Maloney.

•

More tornadoes in the Midwest clearing whole towns flat, but the streets of our little town are peaceful. The little shops and houses and churches and schools.

They have popcorn at the bank on Fridays. Sorority girls are near black from the tanning bed, cashing checks from their daddies. A scout in new boots does *The New York Times* crossword puzzle on a bench in front of the courthouse. A boy calls him Charlie Cheeseburger from across the street. He does tricks with his butterfly knife. Back on the boat, Finger is laughing at a bad sitcom.

It's not that funny, I say.

Yeah, he says, but everyone else is laughing.

There is a man, a born again Christian, on TV who draws perfect circles on a chalkboard, a metaphor for Christ's love. But there is no such thing as perfect, Eli. Someone said once the sunset was perfect and I told him to shut his stupid mouth.

I wish I had a chance to be brave, an opportunity to be a hero. This morning I cared for a sick dying squirrel I hit with my car but it wasn't good enough. I have never delivered a baby in a cab or saved an old man from a river. I want to continue life in a noble way.

A dream: Darling and I are together riding jet skis on Lake Norman, near my childhood home. You are on the shore, Eli, beating Finger in chess and waving the Bonnie Blue. This is a dream but could be life someday.

St. Joan of Arc is raped by an English lord then tied to the stake. She asks the executioner to give her a cross to die with and he fashions one with two twigs.

She was just schizophrenic, you say, Eli.

One man's mental illness is another man's sainthood, I say.

I wonder what she'd been like in the sack?

Definitely a screamer.

She'd bite your head off, man.

Eli, your chess abilities are sharp and we hustle in the park. I'm your barker and manager. I only take 10 percent.

Don't outright beat them, Eli. Let them win a few. That's the hustle.

No mercy, you say. I don't throw matches.

Two wizards watch. You win blitz games against a couple of park regulars and one long game with a twelve-year-old upstart.

People start to huddle around your matches.

One of the wizards climbs a tree.

Are you on the Holy Ghost hit list? Will you be taken down to her river of milk and honey? Darling sighs in the orchard of my dreams. She laughs in that way of hers. The Holy Ghost tickles her toes. We feed each other peaches and moonshine. I gain knowledge of her.

•

Let's talk about the moon, Eli. There are the phases, wax and wane. We sit on the highest hill in town and watch the airplanes.

Ever wish one would crash, I ask.

You got a weird head, Maloney.

No souls lost, Eli, just something to break the silence.

Listen to the words coming out of your mouth, you say.

A bloom of smoke and fire and everyone lives. What a beautiful thing.

You need to go to church Maloney.

I am church, I say.

Finger is doing jumping jacks on the dock. His health is better and he is eating meat again.

I even started smoking, Maloney.

Why?

It makes you tough.

Those things will kill, I say.

All the good people smoke, says Finger. Puts you in touch with death.

I'm in touch with death, I say. It's life I can't get together.

I'm at the Starlight watching Darling pour hot coffee with her perfect pitching arm. She comes over and says there's a call for me. It's Tuesday on the line.

I'm in Bhutan seeking the light, she says. How is Eli?

He is fast on his way to becoming a chess master. Next week we go to the big tournament.

I sent him a wisdom prayer.

Do you pray for me?

It was good to talk to you, she says. Goodbye.

St. William is tied to the stake, strangled and burned. He coined the phrase *Give up the ghost.*

Eli, do you feel alive?

Most of the time.

What about now?

I would say yes. And you?

Can't rightly say.

Another gin?

Why not.

This is what passes for conversation here on the boat.

Eli, you're in the chess club destroying the journeymen. Lots of old wood in this place and paintings that follow you with their eyes. There are some masters here sizing you up. You win one pretty easily but the next one sneaks up on you. Nono is coming to all your chess matches. The tournaments and exhibitions, even park games. She is a small lady with a wild smile. I see her talking to you as I collect your winnings.

What did she want, I ask.

You jealous?

Don't like her moving in on our arrangement.

She's got something, you say. Something unadulterated about her.

Finger is fishing off the boat. He is living with the weather and sun. He's turned away from his freegan principles.

I've forgotten how wonderful money is, he says.

You can be happy without it, Finger.

With cash and a large truck, some diversified assets, a nice little nest egg, I could be happy.

Eli, the couple in my office are the worst parents in the world. They have three children ages one, two, and three. Both are out of work and he wears his boots tucked into his jeans. She wears Playboy bunny pajama pants. She tells me how she dropped two of the babies down some stairs and one is seriously damaged. That's what she says, Eli. Seriously damaged.

In the Starlight, Darling is sweet to me. She serves a man in a neck brace blueberry ice cream. Her hair is cut short for the summer like a French New Wave movie star.

Your legs are graceful, I say.

Thank you.

You have the best kind of eyes.

Thank you.

I want to take you somewhere.

I want to go somewhere.

But we don't move.

4

We're on the train to California for your first pro tournament, Eli. There are all kinds of folks here on the Sunset Limited. Black mothers out of New Orleans, Mexicans and Mennonites from Texas, air force recruits from Nebraska. These people play Go Fish as the nation goes by. Hipsters with tattoo sleeves eat peanut butter sandwiches. Out here, Eli, windmills in the desert do whatever windmills do. I'm filled to the brim today with Jesus and America and Vitamin C.

Should I get beer in the dining car, you ask.

Of course.

You drink sixteen and put them on my tab while I'm asleep. We play chess in the morning and go over your openings. You're in good shape to beat some ass, Eli. We are in America and you will be the greatest.

St. Margaret is of noble birth. A rookie executioner's first blow slices her shoulder rather than her neck. Wounded, she runs. Ten additional blows are required to complete the execution. A wolf licks the blood from the road and stalks the body all the way to the graveyard where he smells the freshly dug earth and runs away.

News from back home. Finger stabbed Dick Dickerson at the pawnshop over the price of a sword. Dick Dickerson saw a woman needed cash.

I'll give you two hundred for it, says Dick Dickerson to the woman.

That sword is worth at least a thousand, says Finger.

Finger, why don't you go do some stocking, says Dick Dickerson.

Well, I need the money, says the woman.

I'll buy it off you for five hundred, says Finger.

You're fired, says Dick Dickerson.

Finger stabs him and walks out.

At least that's how Finger tells it.

There is a voice mail from a man with the U.S. Embassy. Something is wrong with Tuesday. I call back.

Tell it straight, I say.

We're working it out, he says.

What happened? Where is she?

She's in India. Sick.

What kind of sick?

We don't know. They're putting holy candles on her.

Holy candles are the best you got?

Best we got.

•

There are good people in the world and a few bad, but the bad ones get all the coverage, Eli. This is Hollywood. We listen to Sunday church music on the radio. I climb a palm tree and watch the sunset and Tuesday is in some country with no God. The seasons are grinding away and the Holy Ghost is bored. I'm hoping for a miracle or at least a woman with a nice ass to cross the road.

Eli, get your body as ready as your mind. The tournament money is keeping us alive. You drink beer during and wear shades like the poker players on TV. I hold your hat and cigs.

In L.A., there is sad beautiful Hollywood light everywhere. Everyone desperate for something to happen. The pools and drugs. All the cliques inside of clichés. People complaining about how perfect it is. Yoga. Soy iced coffee. Massage and marijuana. The celebrities are boring. The homeless are boring. I love it all, Eli. Great America, ho!

Eli, you've won first place and we hold the trophy high. This newspaperman wants to do a story on you.

Eli, what is your overall strategy?

To kill the king.

What do you say to all those kids out there who want to be a chess champion like you?

Kill the king.

•

Back on the train out the window fireworks bloom from the little towns as we cross through the night, Fourth of July. Look at the lemon groves and the kids playing soccer. The Buckville, Texas, train station is an art deco palace with red stained glass windows. High-back leather chairs in the main waiting room. Birds fly in, sometimes stopping by your chair. A finch on your lap as you wait for the train, maybe you are drinking a martini.

There is a man who claims he's Cherokee. He walks with a stick with a skull on it. He's like Bruce Springsteen when he talks. He has that look of fear.

What do you say there, mister, he says.

I'm here with my friend playing some chess.

Chess, he says. That's all?

Yeah, I say. What do you do?

I find people, he says. I search and I find them.

St. Anne is bound with chains to the stake by her ankles, knees, waist, chest, and neck. She is burned slowly. She does not scream. There is music in her ears from a small boy practicing his flute on a roof in the distance. His mother would not let him go to the execution until he finished his scales.

There is an announcement that a man has offered to entertain the children in the observation car. He is a fat man in a car mechanic's shirt. He's a special effects makeup guy or he wants to become one some day. He paints big gashes and scars.

I was a PA on the movie *Gremlins*, he says to the children.
What's a PA, says a kid.
Gremlins was a very important movie, the man says.
Can you make it look like I killed myself, says a little girl.
Her dress is Wedgewood blue.

A Buddhist monk and a black French Messianic Jew in the
dining car. I say, We're like the beginning of a joke. Miles out
the window. Miles and miles. No one laughs.

It should be required of every young man and woman of
America to travel terrestrially across our great country. For-
ests to desert to plains to mountains to coast. Night comes
quicker out here in the Badlands. One sweet girl in the observation car reads a book I've read. I want to talk to her but
she gets up before I can sit down. I change my shirt. Have a
fantasy about her. We meet. I have a hotel room in New Orleans. Order room service, then get dirty in the shower with
her. She has short hair and glasses. A tiny white scar below
her mouth. I fall asleep and dream of Darling dressed as the
Statue of Liberty.

The special effects makeup man is having a heart attack. They
call for a doctor. Then they call for a doctor or a nurse. They
call for the defibrillator. We back up to the last station and
an ambulance comes. The man is on the stretcher. The sky is
van Gogh chrome yellow. He smiles trying to reassure us, this
makeup man, but he grabs his chest.

The man is dying, says the girl in the Wedgewood dress.

A woman is doing a crossword puzzle and asks, What is the word for "orange" in Spanish?

Gremlins, says the dying man. Was a very important movie.

There is a pregnant woman. She asks other passengers to watch her kids while she smokes. Down in the café car she has a Miller Lite at two in the morning. We are the only two idiots awake.

My husband left me, she says. I'm looking for a strong man with hot hands.

I see.

Hot hands to hold me while I sleep.

I will pray for those hot hands to find you, I say.

What if those hands are yours?

They're not.

The rain's stopped, Eli. I'm in a fog of fantasy. When there is nothing left to do there is memory. All the books read and everyone asleep you can stare out the window and have memories. A woman came in the bookstore I worked at years ago and asked for books on Kenya. She was going on safari. We talked for a while about her son who was a Rhodes scholar and her husband who was an architect. I found her a book and wished her good luck on her trip. That was twenty-five years ago, Eli. I imagine sometimes what her safari was like. I picture her wearing a pith helmet in a jeep watching a lion sleep. Or her eating cantaloupe in a garden served by black men in white uniforms. The sounds of lions killing elephants in the night. I think of her making love to a stranger for the first time in her life and sometimes the stranger is me.

I ask the waitress in the dining car about the white wine. We discuss cork versus twist off. I listen to a sad song on my headphones and dream of a sad movie about two brothers who love the same girl. My belly is full and the green farms go on forever.

They can't get the fire started to kill St. Rowland. He sees this as a miracle. Heaven above will wait for me, he thinks. My prayers are answered. A guard strikes him in the head and kills him instantly. His body is burned anyway.

We finally make New Orleans. All gloom and jazz. New Orleans is the only place left that you can listen to jazz without feeling silly. A coffee shop, Eli, late afternoon. A doctor reads his case files aloud. What disease are you trying to cure?

He shrugs.

All of them, he says.

The day drags on and the place fills up with mysterious people with painted faces. Newlyweds down from Baton Rouge for the weekend to do some shopping mingle among the whores.

I see the girl from the train on the street.

Hey you're from the train, right, she asks.

Yeah, I say.

Would you like to go somewhere and fuck, she says.

Do you believe in God, I say.

No.

I drill her behind a Waffle House.

I hoped for something better, she says.

Don't get much better than that, I say.

Home again. What time is it? Is it time to relax? We shall lift our spirits with some gin and a large left-handed cigarette. Let's throw a party on my party boat. A light cruise up the jetty under the serious stars. Invite all the ridiculous wives and their scotch-smelling husbands and Dick Dickerson and his swinger friends. We will hire a Vanna White look-a-like woman to tend bar.

Where are the people, you ask, Eli.

I wouldn't have come to this party, says Finger, if I weren't already here.

We drive to the all-regional chess tourney in Jackson. There is a man following us in a blue Astro van. When I pass, he passes. He has a small sombrero dangling from his rearview. I try to lose him in my Saab but he keeps coming. We get off at a Wendy's and the man gets off, too. I take a look around. He is wearing a suspicious coat. He's coming toward us.

Eli, get the hatchet.

What hatchet?

Hey, the man says. Hey.

I roll up the window. He taps the glass.

Leave us alone, I say. Get away from the car. I have a hatchet.

You got a damn gas hose stuck in your tank, stranger.

It seems I do.

At the tournament in Nashville, Nono is in the gym eating nachos. She watches your genius with the knights and rooks. This is good money, but this is for the pride, too. A man here with a skull cane and black glasses looks familiar. He nods at me. My spine shivers. I see Nono at concessions. She is beautiful, sixty-five but could be thirty.

I know what you're doing and I don't like it, she says.

What?

You're using him for money.

And what, exactly, are you trying to do?

You'd never understand.

You have no idea how little I understand.

The first rounds are tense. Big dough on the line, old boy. Nervous, Eli? Something is wrong. You blunder in the first round. Why move the knight to king's bishop three? And then again, Eli. You go down in an early mate.

I can't shake it, Maloney.

Shake what?

It's not the same.

This is the match of your damn life, Eli. You can win the big prize and be a master.

I lost it.

Lost what?

All the beauty.

Back home the man calls again about Tuesday.

Things are worse, he says.

What do we do?

There's no way to get back to that remote an area.

What about the army?

They're stretched too thin as it is, Reverend.

What can I do?

I mean short of hiring a helicopter pilot and flying into remote India I don't know.

The Holy Ghost sits on my face. The laws of the spirit, the laws of the dead. Boom wakes me. He is a deputy angel with a bad goatee and elegant shoes. I am needed abroad.

Do you still love her, Darling asks.

Does it matter?

No.

The pilot's name is Snowball, an albino Nigerian. We meet him in a bar outside New Delhi where the cattle roam free as gods. His place is themed as a Wild West joint. The barman wears a ten-gallon hat and pictures of black and white whores line the walls.

Come to my office, Snowball says.

His office is a shrine to Jack Daniel's. Posters, signs, license plates, playing cards, a bar stocked only with the Tennessee sour mash.

We will fly in with an extraction team at zero nine hundred and we'll be in Hamburg by dinner, he says. I charge ten thousand for a day's work.

And what about Jack Daniel's, I ask.

Don't touch anything, he says.

St. Dirk escapes from prison and stops to rescue his pursuer who has fallen in a frozen lake. Then is captured, tortured, and killed.

We fly into the Indian village but the sky could be Texas. A healer meets the helicopter with his palms out, a snake around his neck. He is with a tiny blond missionary who looks like Jane Fonda. We find Tuesday in a sweat lodge in a long robe, so thin her bones are sticking out.

The ghost won't leave her, says a nude villager.

She's been at 103 for five days, says the missionary. She will not last the night.

Snowball says, We leave in twenty minutes. Get her ready.

We load her onto the helicopter. Then the healer flags us down.

Kill the engine, I say.

As the blades come to a stop the healer points his palm toward a cow on the other end of the village. The cow starts to tremble. The healer's hand shakes in the air and then the cow drops dead. He walks to the chopper and lays his hand on Tuesday and she wakes. She steps from the stretcher, walks to a fountain, and takes off her clothes. Bathes to the sound of the villagers cheering. The women cover her in soft linens. Her skin is tan and her eyes are blue again. Healed.

Why couldn't he do that two weeks ago, I say to Snowball. That asshole owes me ten grand.

5

Eli, you've gone to the doctor. You've got high blood pressure, a bad gallbladder, and you need to shed some pounds.

Life's too short, you say, to live too long.

A woman I council orgasms while riding her horse and sitting on her washing machine.

Is this a sin, she says. Am I damned to hell for this?

Not in my book. Jesus was a man who once and a while pleasured himself.

Did he tell you that personally, Reverend?

Yes, ma'am, he did.

Eli, more and more each day I admire your chess. With each match you grow. Your confident openings and elegant end-games. But only in private do you play this well. We play a game.

Who are you, Maloney?

I am a very sick man.
Why do you think so?
Because it's hard to be me.
That's bullshit. Checkmate.

It's spring. The bright golden endless everything. Eli, we have a picnic in the cemetery. There are travelers on their way. We wave and tip our hats to these passersby. We have long lives to live, but some are dealt a shitty hand. Sweet delight, endless night. People died in this town yesterday, but no one died today.

The town is abuzz tonight with boring people. Drunk lawyers talking slow about nothing. A teacher and student laugh about Ernest Hemingway. Two kids play cops and robbers. I notice a book on my shelf that I read all but the last page because I never wanted it to end.

Fly in my coffee so I get some quarters for the paper. There are some town scandals. A greedy billionaire blackmailed a cross-dressing judge. A man grabbed another man in the rain. A disturbed teenage gunman is loose on the streets. All the peace and quiet is gone and I like it.

Eli, Tuesday is coming home today. At the airport she wears a dashiki with her blue eyes. We take the Saab home, Tuesday riding shotgun. The parking lot attendant has teardrop tattoos but a kind face. We go to the good chicken place in the bad part of town. Lone Wolf Spurns Angst, reads a headline in the box. The waitress has a beautiful burn on her neck.

I can get Finger and Eli out and we can have the boat to ourselves, I say.

Finger, Tuesday asks. Who's Finger?

Nono holds a blue umbrella. She is sending you postcards from around the country. What is she trying to pull? I put a pin in the map of each city they come from and it spells out: Eli I love you.

Eighteen monks are hanged, disemboweled while still alive and quartered. The one thing they have in common is their doubt just before the act. We are strangers here, they say. Pilgrims and sinners. Why, oh why, they pray. No one comes to help them.

Eli, how 'bout we go to a wild jungle wearing only loincloths? We can sit and listen to the murder in the trees. Some native girls might swing by. Pineapple umbrella drinks and other delights. We shall raise sails south, ride the river and make New Orleans in two days. Catch a cruise ship to South America. Oh, the birds and the snakes.

Why do we never go, you ask.

You and your questions, I say.

You and your pipe dreams, you say. Castles in Spain.

•

I keep thinking of driver's education class. My driving teacher was a white man named Jesse Jackson. He chewed Red Man and spat out the window. Jackson would say, Slow up. I took us over the hump on Center Street and Jesse Jackson nearly shit himself. He was a bald man of forty-five and his wife did not love him and she went to the airport parking deck and killed herself with a garden hose attached to the exhaust. Memories flood my head. There was the old lesbian librarian that ate alone everyday at Wayne's Restaurant. My weed dealer's name was Clown and he had diabetes. The man-made lake and the bad Chinese buffet. The gone times. I'm too exhausted to sleep.

I am drunk in the doorway of the sanctuary. Ham, the janitor, picks me up.

Maloney, he says. I'm gonna drive you home.

I was good to you, Ham. I brought you and your wife back together.

Then she had a baby with that blind man.

Take me back, Ham. I need to help people.

There is a fine line between suffering and sorrow.

I know, I say. I taught you that.

I watched Satan hand wash his seersuckers in the dark creek near Dead Branch at dawn. Saw the bastard in my scope but couldn't get a clear shot, he was a mile away. We ride, Eli, in Dick Dickerson's Triumph TR3 I hotwired. I'm dreaming we're in Arkansas and Iowa. I bang the Holy Ghost in the hotel bar bathroom.

We should go back to the boat, says Eli.

Let us ride a little longer, I say.

I don't like it here. There's too much mystery in the sky.

Eli, this is the heartbeat of America, long may you run.

This is the shittiest highway in the shitty state.

Take a Xanax, for Christ's sake.

I already took two.

I walk home from the bar in the rain. Ham picks me up again. We ride by my old house, lights are on. I find Finger between Tuesday's legs, eating her. They are on the old piano bench. This was my home with my rundown pool.

Maloney, Tuesday says.

Finger does not stop.

Why this, Tuesday?

We both love you, Maloney, she says.

Finger holds up the love sign. Pointer, pinky, and thumb.

I suggest a threesome but I'm denied.

There is an amazing number of dragonflies out today. Hovering in the yards. A woman won't stop smoking in the non-smoking section of the Starlight. There is much trouble in the world. Listen to the news for ten minutes. But the beer still is delivered and the cars are waxed and people still fall in and out of love. Dick Dickerson is cutting his grass in a puffy blouse.

•

St. Magdalene is suffocated to death suspended upside down in a pit of animal guts on a giblet. She lived with wolves and broke horses in the desert and was a whore in the court of the evil kings of Arabia. She cries at her death and how she had more things to do.

Eli, the chess has come down to the wire and you're all in. I have a lot of cash riding on this, play smart. I see Nono at the back of the gym. She comes over.

What do you have against his happiness, she says.

What do you have against minding your own business?

A family conned my father. This con man was a poor contractor with an ugly, skinny wife. They came to our church and his daughter shit her pants. He drew up blueprints to redo our kitchen. My father wrote him a check for supplies and the guy took his family and left town. But I saw this man again. He had no family anymore. I took him to my chapel. He said his wife died and his daughter ran away. His son was in jail for drugs. He was sorry for everything he'd done to my father. He is now the man at the end of the bar with shaky hands and back pain hitting on the last fat girl in the place.

Eli, where have you gone? Where is the moon? What day of the week was I born on? I'm down in the cabin of the ship playing chess against myself. Trying to think where you would move.

•

I think about all the lost puppies in the world. All those sad endings. There are men here giving firm handshakes to the new guy. What's the agenda for the millions of early morning meetings? How many husbands are right now saying to their wives, I'm sorry I don't love you anymore?

Eli, I knew your sister, Molly. I could never tell you that I loved her once. She was sad and we were on a youth group trip to the woods. I came to her bed in the girl's bunkhouse through the window. I lay with her and felt her breasts and kissed her. She was a kind, slow kisser. It was something I wanted to do over and over. We lay on the grass and synchronized our breathing. I took her breath and she took mine. We were kids, Eli. It was the woods and the darkness and stolen cigarettes. I had no real need for Christ, but he was there swirling around me in the form of doves. Now she is dead, buried on a hillside under a dying oak.

The Mohawks believe St. Isaac practices black magic. They tomahawk him in the neck. His wife is there and embraces him until his body is cold. Then the Mohawk chief takes her to his teepee and shows her his wisdom and she becomes his wife.

Darling wears knee-high socks and roller skates. We go to the all-you-can-eat Chinese buffet out near the crumbling Kmart. There is a Zen river with a tiny bridge and a soft-serve ice cream machine. I have taken many painkillers and have a gin but I am steady. Darling with her sapphire eyes, she is my sweet distraction. Then later, in my arms, she whispers, We're easy as pie.

The Holy Ghost is pale with brown pussy hair. I ride her, watch her breasts bounce in the moonlight. It is dirty but I hold her tender in the sky.

Tuesday and Finger and I are on the boat.
  We've come to tell you we're getting married, says Tuesday.
  Bullshit, I say.
  We want your blessing, Finger says.
  Eli then, no lie, church bells start to ring in the distance.

I've marched into the Starlight and gotten down on my knees and started singing that Righteous Brothers song to Darling. This worked in *Top Gun*, but I am beat up by her father, the owner.
  I only sang to her, I say.
  Why do you have to dress that way, her father says. Why can't you be normal?
  Isn't that the question we're all asking ourselves.
  He punches me in the throat.

I am harassed daily on my bike by a roving gang of fifth graders. Such raw disappointment at every turn. These kids will soon become frat boys then lawyers then alcoholics then die of heart attacks on the golf course with wives they don't deserve.

●

I order a pizza to my boat. The woman driver has a bad smile. She reminds me of the girls that roam behind IHOP. I love her instantly.

You're beautiful, baby, I say.

It's fifteen dollars.

For sex?

For the pizza, asshole.

Soldiers try to shoot St. Devo, but their guns won't fire. He takes their weapons and blesses them and gives them back. They shoot him five times in the face and he dies with the Lord's Prayer on his lips.

I creep up to Darling's place one night and knock on her bedroom window.

Come in, she says. My father's not home.

I climb in. This house has the grand staircase and the high ceilings of the Old South, a big bathroom with a bidet. There's a stuffed tiger in her father's room.

So what do you want to do now, she says.

That's a big tiger, I say.

Yes, it is, she says.

Eli, I follow you and Nono to the movies. I watch from the parking lot with opera glasses I bought at Dick Dickerson's pawnshop. Nono points at the car and you start walking my way. I get out.

What movie are you going to see, asks Nono.

I'm not going to the movies, I say.

Then what are you doing here, she says.

Free country, I say. Then run away.

At the Starlight there's a tourist with a soul patch talking to me about his nude drawings. He is affecting an accent from Eastern Europe. He is here with his lover, a man with tiny glasses. There is a postcard in this town for everything and he has collected them all. The quiet alley where we used to shoot dice is now a Chuck E. Cheese's. What can I do but watch the blond girls with fake tans, fake tits, fake lips, fake hips, fake diamonds, fake everything. But still the sky is pink over the spire of the church and the werewolves lock themselves up at night.

What can I say of Satan, the restless fallen angel warming his hands on a dead man's campfire? Eli, the wizards drink the communion wine. They are father and son. Al and Hal Malchow. They've written a fantasy novel together, though young Hal can barely read.

They throw things at us, too, they say.

Who?

The little preppies on the hill.

St. Baker is killed and eaten in Fiji. His pith helmet falls to the ground and spins in the dust. The locals play drums with his bones. The sky is purple and Bible black. They give thanks to their God and make Baker's killer a saint.

Outside the Starlight the peace is destroyed by a gun-wielding teen. He is high on morphine to ease the pain of killing. A victim to himself. The cops push back the rubberneckers. Maloney, shouts someone in the crowd. You can talk him down.

I get on the bullhorn.

Kid, think about your mother, I say.

Who is that, he says. Who's talking?

I'm the pastor.

My mother said you order sex on the beach shots and sit down when you pee.

The crowd erupts with laughter.

Falsehoods, I say. Put the gun down.

She said you're filthy and you jerk off all day on a boat.

A huge roar from the crowd.

Listen, I say, put the gun down or they're going to shoot your head off.

I'd rather die than listen to this asshole, he says.

A sniper shoots him right between the eyes.

St. Maria is eleven and fights a farmhand from raping her, saying it is a mortal sin. He stabs her and she is operated upon without anesthesia. Her last words are, I will think of you in paradise. Ten angels surround her.

•

The pain is everywhere as I dream on my boat. There is deep sweet melancholy in my slumbering. I see all. I see the wizards near the peach tree. I see Tuesday and Finger laughing on jet skis. I see Bill and Hillary and Monica having a threesome. I see ships in bottles and fields of white cotton. I see the crazed frat boy gunned down in the street. I see the chess pieces falling and the fifth graders with their piss balloons ready. I hear the Sunset Limited round the bend. I see St. Matthew driving my Saab and I see ponies running through the mountains. I see the blossoming of ten thousand wildflowers and the flocking of birds.

Nono comes to the boat. I wake up and there's a cig still burning in my mouth.

I want to tell you about my life, she says.

OK, I say.

I was born in a prison in China and I killed my mother with my birth. When I was fifteen I heard a song by the Beatles on an American channel from Taiwan coming through a guard's radio and dreamed of escaping. After many years of planning, I did escape to Japan on a raft. It took forty-three days and there I married a wealthy architect, but I left him in time. And then I met a famous British actor and moved to Tangier, but left him, too. Finally, I married a starving poet and we lived on the Lower East Side of Manhattan. Then I came to the South to bury my best friend from my days in Africa. I could not heal her so I am staying here, living her life in her honor.

What does that have to do with Eli, I ask.

I love him.

I look at Nono's soft lips.

Why do you love him?

Because I loved a rich man and wasn't happy. I loved a famous man and wasn't happy. And I loved a poor poet and I still wasn't happy. I've gone everywhere, seen everything. Eli makes me happy.

I load a pipe with hash.

6

This hate has gone on long enough, pride is reaching epic levels. These mini bros on the hillside are major mischief-makers countywide, exploring violence and lighting farts. These monsters will grow up to lay off people and beat their children and force them to play sports against their will. I call over an officer of the law.

I am covered in urine from their balloons, officer.

This happens to be my nephew, says the officer.

OK, but I'm covered in urine.

Sounds like a personal problem, he says.

I am a man of the cloth, I say.

He tasers my scrotum.

If a summer day goes wrong it can break you. A girl in Tupelo took an overdose of sleeping pills because her day at the pool wasn't fun enough. But autumn is coming, season of dark poets, my best time. Football will be back and cold beer and pumpkin-launching contests. I will take Darling to the first game in her gingham dress and sweater. We will drink champagne we can't afford at the restaurant we both hate and walk out on the bill. Hail Mary. Hail Mary. Hail Mary. Go team. Go.

I can't read the news anymore. It's a racket, Eli. All I need is the Lord's Prayer and the Pledge of Allegiance and have the band play "Dixie" when I die.

Darling has taken my hand as we walk home and I have taken hers, my heart growing ten thousand. I spend the day cleaning the boat, then drive the Saab to my old house where the tall grass grows around the For Sale sign. I drive to the country to see the cotton. Wise Jane gardens in the pleasant morning in her van Gogh straw hat. We talk flowers.

These flowers, she says, are called naked ladies. When you pick them they make a good noise.

How do I do it?

You snap their necks.

Wise Jane has a pot of the good chicory coffee and her sweet dog Willie is at my knee.

What happens when they all run out on you, Wise Jane? I thought I used to know.

St. Elizabeth is shoved into a pit of snakes by soldiers. They throw grenades in the pit, but hear her singing hymns. They throw three more but she still sings. Finally they set her on fire. The snakes crawl into the woods and breed more snakes and the snakes grow to eat soldiers' children in their sleep.

·

I go to Tuesday and Finger's new apartment on the north side and watch them through the window. It is a comfortable condo with brand new carpet and a video game room. Tuesday has given over to the money now like Finger. She wears furs and high heels and eats at restaurants with no prices on the menus, like the one with the shark tank. Finger sells stocks online and plays high-stakes poker in Atlantic City. I call Tuesday.

Remember when we made love in the sanctuary, I ask her.

Yes, she says.

I hang up.

You could count the bricks in the schoolhouse, Eli. It was something to see. No one taught you anything, you just read Shakespeare in the basement with a joint in your lips. The bad boys put your head in the toilet and made you tongue-kiss a dog. And the teachers slapped you across the mouth for writing with your left hand. Remember, Eli? Remember Mulberry Street School and the tiny room where they put the kids like you?

I dream the Holy Ghost drives a bus while I give her head. I dream about an accountant in a Wild West town twirling his empty pistols for the love of a girl who's run away with an outlaw. I dream all the doctors heal and the firemen fight fires and the policemen police and the nurses nurse and the wrestlers wrestle and the dog sitters sit and the kidnappers nap.

·

I see the teenage electric fiddle player who plays the Beatles. She's in college now with large breasts that do not sag. She loves an MMA fighter with tattoos covering him. This man is unemployable with his face full of ink. A gentle man who likes to hear the crack of bones. I'm doing the backstroke now in the ice-cold water under a faint day moon with my eyes full of the red vineyards of France. I never told you but I have dreams of going there. To the place where love began.

Al and Hal the wizards are here. They hate the pain of this world so live in another. I envy their happiness with fantasy and play.

Hello, Al, I say. Hello, Hal.

Maloney, we've got a battle plan.

I am at a banquet with ghosts. White Mike Johnny and the frat boy with the gun are pouring wine for everyone. John Lennon and Joan of Arc bicker about the kind of turkey Napoleon bought. There are peaches everywhere. I am waist high in peaches. Boom is seated at the head of the table with his prayers and his pony.

I've got kids raining pee down on me, Boom, I say.

Every woman's a feminist until they need a jar of pickles opened, he says.

What does that mean?

Money, says Boom.

Money?

Dick Dickerson comes to the boat with a loaded .45. He has no real talents or memories or cares. He's gone on junk and Everclear.

I want Tuesday, Dick Dickerson says pointing his weapon.

Well she ain't here, I say.

Declare God doesn't exist or I'll kill you, he says.

I take his gun with judo and make him walk the plank.

I come to the Starlight for the first time in months and prop my boots up on the table.

You're not allowed in here, the cook says.

I love you, I say. I wish I could remember your name.

My father was a famous eye man, looked into the soul for a living. My mother a sweet librarian who hid the dirty books on the top shelf. A man orders a latte but he pronounces it luh-tay. The radio keeps predicting rain but there is never rain. Darling is on my mind now. Her sapphire eyes.

St. Miguel's last request is to be allowed to pray as doves swoop down and touch his lips. The firing squad shoots him twelve times but he won't die. They put a bullet in his head and as it passes through he thinks of a little girl he saw eating ice cream on a winter day and how stupid and courageous she was.

•

I'm up in a tree with my opera glasses, scratching my balls, waiting. Down below the middle schoolers reveal themselves. I watch them stalk their victims. Like in nature, they prey on the weak. A kid in a neck brace with a lisp is in their crosshairs. They shoot M-80s at him till he falls and they steal his Subway sandwich. One of the bullies has a popped collar and a silver watch and the hair of Matt Damon. Then I see Dick Dickerson. What is he doing? He talks to the boys and points around. A yellow Hummer rounds the corner playing Aerosmith. He gets in.

Eli, I watch you and Nono through the window of her organic market. You seem happy, content. You are my friend and she is your lover. What's my problem with other people's happiness? I see you dancing, I see you eating pink beet soup. Why can't I have this ease, Eli? I stalk Tuesday and Finger, too. They are playing Xbox and smoking bongs. Jumping on the bed with joy. Darling catches me in the tree looking in their house.

What's up, doc, she says.
I fall out of the tree.
Darling, what are you doing here?
I've been stalking you.
Stalking me? Why?
I might be in love with you, she says.
Good to hear, I say.

The days pass without much terror. I'm content with my ship and its amenities, microwave, cable TV. Darling makes me breakfast and I smoke my pipe. It's good to be out of bed and in the air again watching the birds eat the fish and the hawks eat the birds. We go to town in the Saab and buy things from the market. Taking a woman to a market to buy fresh food is the right thing to do. In the parking lot on the way back to the car, I hear something over my shoulder.

Maloney, the voice says. It's Dick Dickerson. I have Eli.

Have him?

He's in my basement. Tuesday, too.

St. Toro is shot by soldiers, falling into his sister's arms, saying, Long live Christ the King. He is deaf and the stars become his ears.

Finger and Tuesday's condo, new shag carpet and a Lamborghini in the garage. I knock on the door and when Finger opens it he punches me in the face.

You took her, he says.

It's Dick Dickerson. He's taken Eli, too.

Why should I believe you?

Why would I come here if I had taken her? To get my face punched?

I've got my plans spread out on the table in the breakfast nook. Darling is on the deck nude, trying to rid her bikini line. She is a kind, petite brunette. Her eyes are the color of Starry Night, her long brown legs won't quit. She's had no college education but won't stop reading everything she can. This summer she took down the big Russian novels and the French poets. Finnegans Wake in two weeks.

I think I've almost figured all this out, she says. Joyce is overwrought. Faulkner is sappy. Nabokov, a confusing bore. Hem-ingway, a closet homo. Fitzgerald, don't get me started.

Darling, we've got to get to work if we're going to save ev-eryone.

OK, she says, let me finish this chapter.

Eli, Dick Dickerson has you but don't worry. The stars and moon are lining up and the baffling roads are leading some-where. Yes, Eli. Do you feel a bit of the sword that pierced His side in you? Some of Adam's rib? Some of Eve's naughty mouth? The thud on Goliath's head? Do you hear the confus-ing music of God's love played from David's lute?

I go to Al and Hal. They are playing some infernal video game about conquering lands and defeating kings.

What the hell is this, I say.

You have to try it, Hal says.

Dick Dickerson has Tuesday and Eli.

They lower their hoods.

Let's get to work, I say.

Darling is a French Jew filtered through generations of red-neck and Aztec. You can still see that darkness in her skin. Love is poached eggs and the Sunday newspaper and slow, hard sex.

Maloney, what if we do nothing, Darling says.

What do you mean?

What if we didn't go after them? Isn't that what he wants us to do?

I don't follow you.

We could be together on the boat and leave Eli to escape.

I look out over the water. Darling is dark and good.

Give up the pilgrimage? The rescue? Sainthood?

Yes.

Too late, I say. It already happened. It's always been happening.

I wait to enter the Holy Ghost until the sun goes down behind the black hills. There are diamonds in her eyes. There is blood on her tongue. Darling is there with her robin's blue dress and hood of white.

You will have a child, she says to Darling.

What if I don't believe in you, Darling asks.

You don't have to.

St. Arnold writes a letter to his family the night before he is beheaded and tells them to give his prized donkey to the people of the village and his prayer rug to the beggar and his sandals to the washerwoman. The next day the letter is burned with all his effects and his head is cut clean off.

The world drifts back into football season. All the good colors are back, strawberry and chrome yellow and Carolina blue.

The coeds have broken out the fur boots and let their pussy hair grow. We have a planning meeting for the mission to rescue you, Eli. Nono and Finger and Al and Hal and Darling.

Let's call the cops, says Finger.

We should try talking to him, says Nono.

Spells, say Al and Hal.

I want to go back to the boat, says Darling.

I give the St. Crispin's Day speech from Henry V and everyone leaves the room.

The night before the raid I am somber. Reflecting, I lie on my boat with my fisherman sweater and pipe. I dream of a city, Eli. A city where everyone has a beautiful car. Not like this town we live in, Eli. It's destroyed us slowly, bit by bit. I dream of this city where there are no firemen because the fires put themselves out. Where there are no ambulances because all the people heal themselves. Where there is no illness of the mind. There are only longings in this city. Longings to be back where the old world was broken. Where sin surrounds everything. In this city I dream of, no one wears their sunglasses inside. I am the black sheep of dark horses. You are Eli, my last friend.

I call Snowball, the albino.

How fast can you get to Mississippi, I say.

How much you got?

Last of my savings, five thousand.

For five grand I'm free on Friday.

•

Eli, the cafés are empty and red leaves are everywhere and the trees are full of lightning and we are stealth in the night. I have stolen a horse and rented a Confederate general costume from the Halloween store in the poor people's mall. We gather at Nono's and have wheatgrass shots. Synchronize your watches, friends. I have my rifle with scope, Finger has his pawnshop sword. Nono has organic pepper spray and Al and Hal have robes and long wizard staffs. Darling is in the corner.

I don't like this, she says.

Take a grenade.

Why should I?

What's it gonna take?

I make tender love to her but nothing helps.

Twelve-year-old St. Marie's parents poison her for proclaiming Christ was the father of her child. They shove the poison down her throat. She made ballerina shoes all day and saw the light of Christ in a thimble. She wasn't a virgin anymore. The father was a Romanian man from the traveling show. She wanted forgiveness for the baby inside her and she begged for it as she closed her eyes and swallowed.

Eli, we're at the lower soccer field at the middle school. Al and Hal get in the hot air balloon piloted by Snowball. They put up the hoods of their robes. I give them the thumbs-up.

See you on the other side, I say.

Dick Dickerson lives in a compound. The sun is starting to creep below the hills looking like a thrift store painting. I ride up on my horse. I have named him Forever. Through my opera glasses, the house is quiet. I call Finger from my radio.

I'm nearing the door now, he says.

Go, I say. All go.

Two flares go off from the hot air balloon and I put some heavy fire on the house. Snowball drops the rope. Al and Hal repel down into the courtyard. I see a light in the window.

Eli, the heavens are open with loving blue pouring down. All the days of the calendar spiral and bend. We are weak, loving warriors doing our best. There will be a child, says the Holy Ghost. A child to save America. She must be born inside the lady of freedom.

There are mortars flying from the windows and Snowball is dropping bombs from the balloon. Fire at will. Finger is pinned down behind an old sharecropper's cabin. I ride Forever through the gate and Nono and the Malchows flank right. There, in the top-floor window is Dick Dickerson with his robe open and his privates flapping in the night. I fire off three rounds but he vanishes behind the velvet curtains. Here come the bullies out the door, Eli, and I put some rubber bullets along their chests. One gets a throwing star off and it whizzes by my face so close I feel the breeze. Al and Hal come in with their staffs and hold them down and cast spells.

Finger, have you found anything, I call.

There is a whole mess of rooms in this place, Reverend, he says.

I ride Forever through the front door.

Dick, I shout. Give it up.

Fighting surrounds the house. Windows breaking and the red shrieking bombs. Dick Dickerson appears at the top of the stairs nude. There is the smell of gasoline.

Maloney, he says. So glad you could make it.

What do you want, I ask.

I want the love you have, he says. The fire you have.

He walks down the stairs and begins to play Bach on the piano. Then lights a match and the whole house goes up.

Forever and I ride out into the flaming night.

The whole neighborhood burns. I watch the McMansions come down. Beside me is Finger, former dumpster diver turned stockbroker. Next to him is Nono, a woman of great adventure. And then Al and Hal, former wizards, who finally felled their bullies. Where's Snowball, I ask.

Got a little rocky up there, he says from behind me. Had to bail.

I give him a hit from the pint of Jack Daniel's in my general's coat.

The good stuff, he says.

Where's Eli and Tuesday, Nono asks.

I don't know, I say.

Eli, I scream. Tuesday!

Then a sound. Is that you, Eli? A low howling coming from the deep woods. We all run to an open patch. You are standing there holding Tuesday's hand.

Where have you been, Eli?

Looking at the moon, you say.

7

The days are shorter and the Confederate daughters weep under men on stone horses. A hurricane named Honey is swirling off the gulf. When you were gone, Eli, I smashed all my ships in a bottle. Out there above the cotton are dead stars whose light we still see.

Virgin birth can scientifically happen. But this means nothing. Or it does but I don't know what it is. Christ said there would be no more kings but there were kings.

Tuesday comes to the boat, Eli. She is with child and wears a ring from Finger. They were married on a weekend to Gatlinburg.

Thank you, she says.

For what?

You took me from the brink, you taught me.

Tuesday, I was grasping in the dark.

And you loved me and I spit it back in your face.
I know, I say.
She comes to me and is warm there in my arms, forgiven.

They cut the bottom of St. José's feet and make him walk toward the cemetery. He does not give in. At times they stop him and say, If you shout Death to Christ the King, we will spare your life. José only shouts, I will never give in. Moments before his death he draws a cross in the dirt and kisses it. In the town square is a girl jumping rope and a butcher draining blood into the street. The girl trips and the daisy falls from her hair into the blood. The yellow trees shiver in the yard and the dog's barks sound like I love yous.

My boat rocks in the water. I am moving through the world in my mind. Intellectuals destroyed the imagination and Christians destroyed the fun.

There's a knock at the door. It's Darling. She's angry but still has the smile from deep within. There are strawberries on the table in a cold white bowl.

I came to get my things, she says.
She gathers her lace underwear and records and books.
I'd like to start over if I could, I say.
Start what over?
Everything.

•

The firemen are testing their fire trucks shooting water all night like a waterfall of diamonds. The marching band on campus plays "Bang a Gong." There is a bit of hope left, slim as it may be. Elvis died on the crapper, they say. John Lennon gunned down in the street. It doesn't matter where and when you die, Eli, it matters how you get there. I see Finger on the street with his new suit and short hair.

Hi, Finger, I say.

He laughs.

I think I'm going to play pool at that bar, he says.

OK, I say.

We challenge the girls in tight jeans to a twenty-dollar game and let them win. I put a quarter in the jukebox. We drink whiskey sours. There is sun in the forecast.

St. Bart goes to the firing squad barefoot in order to be more conformed to Christ. A doctor to the poor, he even once saved the life of his future executioner. This is a country with no money and beautiful trees. The cherry blossoms rain down on the executioner's face and he wipes them away.

I go to Nono's market to buy flowers for Darling and there you are, Eli.

Good morning, I say.

Morning, Maloney.

Eli, how are you?

Good, how are you?

I'm well, Eli.

There is a pause.

You laugh. I laugh. We laugh. I'm not really sure why we are laughing but we are laughing.

The Holy Ghost licks me head to toe. I want to ask her questions but I'm mute with pleasure. There are doves flying out of my heart in figure eights.

Eli, your wedding to Nono is a sight. You ride Boom's pony down the aisle and Willie dog is the ring bearer. Wise Jane makes some sort of psychedelic hooch and we enter the other side with love on our minds and eat ourselves stupid. Romantic spells are placed upon bride and groom by Al and Hal. Tuesday and Finger make love under a dogwood like it was the first time the act was ever performed. Darling is in the corner of the field looking north to a great unknown like a moonstruck goddess.

8

You've reached the voice-mail box of Reverend Maloney—well-tempered cavalier and reluctant spiritual guide, first mate on Christ's holy ship and lover of females in every state of the former Confederacy. I'm usually tripping the light fantastic on Wednesdays so I might not return your call till Thursday. Have a blessed day—leave a message after the beep.

Beep.

Sir, this is the Lafayette County sheriff. Seeing if you wouldn't mind coming down to talk about the disturbance at Dick Dickerson's last week. We're two doors down from First Baptist across from the Afro-American's barbershop. Thanks.

Eli, your dear friend and supporter is summoned by the powers that be. Might there be an escape on the horizon?

You should learn something about the right to remain silent, you say.

Silent, I say, is not my normal position.

•

The rains come quickly in the fall like a silver curtain drawing closed at the end of a beautiful play. Battleship clouds over a small layer of thin blue. A purple twisting wind like a river, right over the house, threatening. Darling enters stage left in the drama of my life.

I'm pregnant, says she.

Well, well, well, I say.

That's it? That's your response?

Well, well, well, well, well.

Here the will of God is done as God wills as long as God wills. St. Gerard is bilocated preparing Darling a little office of our lady at the same time he crosses the red vineyard praying in the room of tears. America of iron and steel, America of rivers and trees, America of digital hearts and minds. There comes unto you a child.

Gazing into the abyss, I try to keep my balance. Bishops of the night, hear my heart as it goes out into the rattling darkness of the city to dream unspeakable things. The Holy Ghost strokes my loins and we engage thousands of mystics in prayer.

Ramshackle police station in the center of town. A coffee-stained table and a one-sided mirror in a small room like every noir movie. Sheriff cleans his glasses with his tie.

Do you know why you're here, Reverend?

A disturbance at Dick Dickerson's, as I understand it.

There's six witnesses saying you're at the scene riding a horse around in a general's uniform, firing at will.

Allegedly.

A female cop hunches over with a tit half hanging out.

A whole subdivision was burned to the ground, says she.

I believe there was a kidnapping and I was a hero, I say.

I see no heroics here, says the sheriff.

Am I under arrest?

Get out of my office, Maloney. But don't leave town.

St. Wolf sees blue mountains in his dreams and rides the serpent into the shadows. A bullet strikes his heart but he knows how to fly. Guide me, great magic, he says. The great magic says nothing.

They say there is a man who will chase you like a prophet. He plays the sixty-four black and whites well. I feel him watch me without eyes. There is an island of millions and I am the swallower of millions and the millions swallow me. The dead keep dying but their watchmen go on watching. There is a lady who stands in a harbor and she holds a torch against the night.

What the hell is this all adding up to, you say, Eli.

I'm a reluctant pilgrim in all this, I say. Trying to pull my weight.

Vanity. All is vanity.

I saw that written on a wall somewhere.

I wrote it there.

•

Darling rides shotgun in the Saab. I am lost in the wilderness of my mind, climbing up the ladder but standing still. I read the gospel in the shade to her in search of a remedy. I hold a dead magnolia blossom like a hand grenade.

As I see it, she says. It can't go on living if we go on living this way.

I curl Darling's dark hair around her teeny ears.

Look out at the flowers and squint, I say. It's as if the sun has blossomed.

Fuck you, she says.

I spend the day on deck getting my body burned red as a schoolgirl's blush. Down on my hands and knees with no protection whatever—completely nude. I find there is a new blue to the sky or perhaps an old blue newly available to my eyes. And then a night so dark I get erections till dawn.

The Holy Ghost is a white-hot angel as she rides me. Freckles splashed across her face like constellations. Her red lips grasp my dick. I let the horses in my heart run wild.

Al and Hal Malchow seek justice on the Internet for victims of rape wearing Guy Fawkes masks. They read the message boards and know where the pedophiles are. We have a couple cups of hot black coffee down at the Starlight.

Are you happy, Maloney, they ask.

It depends on what your definition of happy is, I say.

•

Darling's showing me pictures of a burning mattress. She's now taking photos of the world around us. Her thoughts have quieted and her eyes are strong.

I want to document things on film, says Darling. Arrest time.

Why?

So she can see what the world was like before she was born.

You went to the doctor?

Yes.

A she, really?

We're having a girl.

She will be the new Christ child for America.

The chickens are out pecking the yard. The gay couple, Kurt and Courtney, farm organically. Doing their part to save what's left of the dying world. Lovely friends, they give us eggs.

Why chickens, I say.

We ordered ducks but they sent us chickens, they say.

I see.

But we love the chickens, says Courtney.

Hell, we love everything, says Kurt.

Sheriff at my door, Eli. Big shadow on the floor. I am drunkenly grooming my pubic hair in the shape of a cross in the boat's tiny bathroom.

Maloney, shouts the sheriff.

You got a warrant, I say.

I got some handcuffs and a .45.

Give me a minute.

Then the sheriff is slamming my bathroom door, fists raging.

I jump out the oval window and swim for it. Steal a jet ski from a random dock and ride through the dying sun on the water. I ditch the machine in a cove, masturbate to my acumen of escape, cum on some poison ivy, and head to town.

Darling sleeps on my chest, her belly growing a person that is half me. I am holed up in her apartment till I plan my next move. She takes her lithium with cinnamon tea.

Why did you come all the way here, says she, dozing.

I've found myself in love with you and I'm on the lam.

I've decided to have the child in New York, Maloney. And I want you to take me there.

I'll take you there, baby, I say.

9

Manhattan bound with my sailboat hitched to the back of our Saab convertible. We breach the Mississippi line, an uncommon family on a strange vacation. Darling dyed her hair jet white and is beginning to show our child in her belly to the world.

Mothers are like oceans, Darling says, and their children are like islands.

Fathers are geology, I say.

Danger abounds. Suddenly there is nothing but a world of clouds and snowy hills and whispers. Eli, you must join the quest, your grandfathers are calling you. Take these arrows, take this bow. Your dead brother's blood will rush in you like the mighty Mississippi.

Why does your heart speak so strangely, you say, Eli.

The dream is marvelous and the terror is great.

Out here on the road my visions are fevered. A legless woman in the street says she's seen the face of all faces. I have my collapsible long rifle and scope in my briefcase with the ivory handles. My hair slicked back for effect. When was the last time you saw the devil, I ask the legless woman. What color was his tie?

The paper rose in his lapel was wilting from the monsoon, she says.

And were his eyes dark, I say. Did he touch you?

This legless lady, Eli, she blows a kiss to me.

St. Dietrich plots to assassinate the dictator and fails. He's hanged and his faithful horse rides off into the hills full of olive trees. The horse lives with a traveling show and one night thieves cut out the ringmaster's tongue. The sand sings in the dunes and the horse runs forever in the darkness.

Let's put physics in reverse, Eli. Use an event horizon as a glory hole. Jump the turnstile to the dimension where Boom is still alive. Maybe there's a world where we are kids playing doctor with the neighborhood girls again. Tiny adventures to please our dirty minds. Our souls age at a cosmic pace.

Out the car window is our wild fantastic country, rolling on. Quick prayer for the Indians. Let them have the sweet rain they're always dancing for. I drift, reckless as we ride. The old Kentucky roads of my youth under our wheels. The ponies I straddled here, Eli. Have I told you? I had a horse and a princess and an electric city constantly unreachable in my dreams.

I was a ballerina as a girl, Darling says. Heel, toe. Pirouette.

I can see you there in my mind, I say. The delicate rising of your leg to the bar.

There was a peculiar sadness when I danced, she says. There was an elegant sorrow as I vaulted through air.

I long to live with eyes like smoke. The whole sweet science— I see it. History is breath against breath. Puff puff, blow the house down. The falling walls of Jericho. The crumbling towers in lower Manhattan. Dick Dickerson's house becoming ash. I kiss Darling like a madman, raise my hand to the night, and ask the Lord a question. Where are you, Señor Cloak and Dagger? Hosanna in the highest, if that's your real name.

Dying is living for me. Our child grows as we fade. Inside Darling's belly she is the size of a fist. We blaze a straight shot up through the guts of America aiming for the grey girl on her island.

Satan was seen buying a café au lait on Friday the thirteenth in the Year of the Dog. He was wearing a Mexican wrestling mask and a monocle on a gold chain the color of the sun. The lights of the casinos filled his good eye. Our days are numbered, our weeks are fading away.

He is blind, this man I see. He is of indeterminable ethnicity, he wears Hawaiian shirts and smokes a cigar like a woman. Exact replicas of his eyes are tattooed on his eyelids. Red laces on his hobnail boots. Are we to trust this man's ability to search and destroy us? Nono has hired him to find you, Eli. She has made him a thermos of soup. He is the copilot of their minivan. His name is Jack Cataract.

These are the years of recklessness and pride. We are the sinners barely comforted by Christ. Let us seek the strong hand of Mister Unknown. Eli, we have driven out the demons of lesser men. We have fought the tough battles on the sixty-four black and white squares. My aging Tonto. My mystical amigo, we ride on.

St. Walter dies in a fire but they say he walked on water. The moon is a Cheshire cat above the palm trees, dancing. Put the lilies in a basket, are his final words.

We have a midnight loiter in the dunes, Darling and I. The American sky is black with expanding stars, one could call it dignity. We are on the threshold to happiness outside the laws of man. Sexual congress with urgency like it's the end of days. When it's over she's got that good light inside once again.

I was a whore and you brought me in, she says. I had all seven sins.

You were a waitress at Starlight when I met you.

I love you deep as an ocean, she says.

High as a mountain, I say.

10

Blazing up through the Appalachians I feel Nono and Cataract at our backs. Hellhounds on our trail in a brown minivan. I belt out a song from my youth, "Ten Little Indians." What vibes up here in the north, Eli. The Civil War left a weird suture along the gut of the country.

We are far from our comfortable Southern despair now as the city lights approach. Manhattan is a sparkling sickness of an island. Condos made for Euro trash, swimming pools in the sky. Over the bridge, Eli, here we come. I'm your incognito kemosabe, you're my redneck Virgil. Graveyards on top of graveyards and where the hell do we park this boat?

East Village, but where are the poets and punks? A KFC on the corner and every man a smiling wad of cash. All the starving artists eat well by professionally wringing their hands on the Internet. Everyone is an extraterrestrial here. My poverty of spirit has returned. Downcast eyes and a desire for prescription painkillers.

Washington Square to hustle the hustlers. The standard players playing five-dollar games. The big guns playing twenty bucks. A couple young Bobby Fischer posers with their mothers eat baloney raw. I buy a joint off a thin black kid named Fuck Face and Darling and I fire up as you collect winnings, Eli. Then I am struck with a vision. Cataract smoking a blunt with the pages of the Book of Revelation. His eyes have never seen a woman or an ocean. Darling watches a skywriter propose marriage in the air. Horrible music plays from horrible cars.

Darling, come closer. We are high on the rooftop where we sleep.

There are four million possible earths out there, I say.

Yes, but also black holes everywhere, she says.

Goldilocks planets, they call them. Not too hot, not too cold.

Darling's ears are cool to the touch.

Maybe each star is a little bonfire on the beaches of heaven.

She touches my nose. We kiss.

Some kid trapped between the wall up in Queens sings the Bee Gees till he's found. Women apply lipstick in the reflection of the butcher shop window. A man walks in tap shoes down the street. A girl pukes out of a cab. A dog licks another dog's vagina. These are weary days as we walk the streets. Laying low for fear of the fuzz. Wanted posters of us all over town.

Eli, I tuck you in on the boat parked near Union Square. There is a circus, a clown, a dwarf, and his gimps.

Armadillos have the most attractive dreams of any animal, you say, Eli.

I'm thinking of living underground, I say. Where no one would find us. I would drive the trains.

I saw a man once crying down there playing cello, you say, Eli.

To be in the darkness for so long underground as I drive, I say. Then to come up from the tunnel into the light. It's got to be something like birth.

Yes, says Darling. But wouldn't the light hurt your eyes?

We've taken up residence in St. Thomas Church on Twelfth Street downtown, closed for repairs. Eli, you sleep in the belfry, we put two pews together. The stained glass windows make our faces blue.

St. Zim refuses to spit on a picture of Christ and is beaten to death in a stadium in front of ten thousand people. It is the largest public gathering in the city in some time.

Darling is bundled up like a child in swaddling. She wears a leopard-print hood and a cashmere scarf stolen from a frazzled heiress. Yes, we go to the jazz club and I commandeer the piano. Kick up my leg and piss my pants while playing "Great Balls of Fire." These bouncers touch my Darling. There is a row. When the man's fist collides with my face, it feels as if it were meant to be. Angels from heaven surround me like a Saturday morning cartoon. When I wake up Darling is screaming.

How could you get beat up like that? They could've found us.

She slaps me and I'm all question marks.

In New York people rap to themselves as they walk down the street and the florists look at naked pictures on their phones. Love is everywhere and we feel it but we can't see it. It's a child's concept of God. Fill my lungs with the breath of life. Put Christ's blood in my blood, his flesh in my belly. Let us eat God clean and pick our teeth with His bones.

There are strange beauties everywhere. A whole pack of models stroll down Houston. A woman is a tailor. A man sells European shoes. His ascot is a handsome teal. We drink rum and toast to a fair fucking fine howdy-do.

A toast to all the wars we've won and lost, the Englishman says.

To all the deaf people, I say, and the people who've been bitten by rattlesnakes or probed by aliens or fondled by their uncle or ever had their wisdom teeth taken out or had appendicitis, to all the people who died virgins, to all the people who don't know how to drive stick. Blessed be to God.

Rev. Maloney, drunk as hell, says you, Eli.

Sometimes I feel like we're soldiers but there's not a war.

Darling cuts a lime slice for my beer.

I love her.

11

I'm the mayor of a lonely country. A passenger on wax wings tilting left to right, diving toward a river as the peasants go about their day. Another politician is found with his dick in his hand, a belt tight around his neck. I scratch the scratch-offs and play the numbers, the ponies, the fights. There are longer shadows later in the day. Darling takes my hand.

I want so bad to be a saint but I'm a coward and barely Christian, I say.

That makes you a good candidate, she says.

The urbanites dress like sinners and I love the sin. I rank folks mainly by their vice and folly. A blond with daddy issues sucks heroin up her nose. Hurt me, Lord, she says, I want to feel more nightmare. I seek the love of the Trinity but there is only my DNA, my center of gravity, my supercilious mouth. I step to the edge of the roof.

What are you doing, asks you, Eli.

Feeling the pull.

Thinking of cashing in, are you?

I've already done that, Eli. I'm just waiting for the horses to carry me away.

For millions of years no creature had an eye. When did life start eating itself, growing as it diminished?

We are born to eat each other, I say.

But we have hearts and brains and courage, Darling says.

The baby kicks in her belly.

What color was the first eye, Darling asks.

Manhattan is a place where all spirits go to die. My mustard seed of faith can move no mountains here. I take the elevator to the top of the Empire State. It is the godly cock of the island, reaching heavenward. The Chrysler is the godly cock of art. The Freedom Tower is the godly cock of grief. I will soar between them with my homemade wings. Nono irons Cataract's shirt in a fleabag motel. He makes instant coffee and plays computer chess. Everyone on daytime TV is a psychopath.

Two NYU bros argue over the best cut of steak, grass-fed or kosher. A maid vacuums a dead man's hair from a motel bed. Nothing in this city can be thrown away. Every sin settles in your heart forever. I seek the right questions that will make the silent Father speak. The Holy Ghost tells me I'm an elephant killed by a small arrow.

I'd like to die and live forever, I say.

Or give your life to someone else, says Darling.

I touch her forehead.

You're warm, I say. You should lie down.

Does the Lord suffer, too? Does he have woe? The Krishnas and Adventists throw their hands up in Union Square. The happy throngs, Eli, full of love and misery. We hustle chess on this old sunny day but then a thin kid puts a knife to your throat.

I thought this was a safe city now, I say to him.

It was till whites started killing brothers.

I have Cherokee blood, I say.

Everybody says that, he says.

Yeah, everybody says that, I say.

Give me the cash, says the kid.

I give him my money and my rabbit's foot and dagger.

I have no answers for the fading American empire. The streets are quiet now but souls are heavy with gold or the anger that comes with too much hunger. Cataract scouts furniture for his dream house. This might be a good place for him to settle down once his mission is complete. I go to the Met and take my time. It is my church, my house of worship. To the Japanese garden on the second floor.

Damn, this shit is tranquil, says the woman with the purple hair.

It's Zen, I say.

Tranquil as hell, she says.

•

I build my wings in the basement of St. Thomas Church. A cigarette between my lips and some hymns playing low on the boom box. The ATM signs make whores' faces red and the crusty kids from Idaho stay warm cuddling black labs with red bandannas. An old man in his underwear runs after a girl with diamonds in her ears. Then to my personal heaven. I rock Darling in my arms after a long day of work. Flesh of my flesh, I say.

You really think I came from your rib, she says.

I don't care where you came from baby, I say. I'm just glad we're here.

On the subway I catch the eye of a girl who looks like Tuesday with a man who looks like Finger. I run for them but they get off the train. I squeeze my way through the doors but my leg is stuck. A drunken lacrosse team pushes me out just before I'm sliced in half. I run after Finger and Tuesday. I knock over a German tour group and nearly push a blind babushka onto the rails but save her at the last minute. I run up the stairs. I can feel Tuesday and Finger's comfort again. Their friendship. Their weirdness.

Tuesday, I call. Finger!

A man dressed as a woman and a woman dressed as a man turn around.

Sorry, I say. Thought you were someone else.

The summer fades to leafless trees and the rapists on Rollerblades fill the parks again. Cops' walkie-talkies bark out numbers and a drunk girl is always crying in the street.

I lost my dog, she says.

What's the name?

Mr. Nobody.

Nobody?

She weeps.

Nobody. Nobody. Nobody.

I am among the long-distance runners in the long-distance race. They enjoy their strong hearts. They say running gives them great sexual pleasure.

Where are we running, I ask a runner.

To the finish line.

Where's that?

Depends on how far you want to go.

St. Edmund dies in the arms of a peasant girl. He's known for wearing shirts made of human hair. Tonight at St. Thomas Church we dine on rotten peaches and stale coffee, Eli. I shall set sail into the great expanse of sky and to that Lady Liberty and fill the voids of my heart with a new child for the nation. I am the wings, bad saint of the sky. I am the lover of wonders. Peace be with you.

And also with you, you say, Eli.

Go back to sleep, I say. There's nothing good out here to report.

From sea to shining sea, lift up thine eyes. To the serious nurses going serious places. To the asinine lovers of fine wines and cigars and the food-obsessed. There is nothing worse than an aficionado. Darling, come closer to me and let my hand rest on your belly. Just a little and let's weep together for this the most awful and beautiful nation in history. The stranger asks the stranger, Will you watch my stuff? I fall in and out of love with humanity again and again. A cop kills an unarmed kid. Hate. A Korean wedding party laughing on a double-decker bus. Love.

St. Charles dies in the dunes of Arabia holding the hand of a lost rabbi. They pray together to the same God in different ways. They feel the pull of the long-dead kings of the world, their slaves and wives and plagues and firstborns murdered in the streets. Eli, we could eke out some romantic vision of the South, go back to the old time religion of Mississippi. Stay closer to the cave than the drawing room. Destroy the poets with their hearts on their sleeves.

Cataract reads Penthouse in braille. He writes songs about the rapture on his yellow guitar. Nono jogs in her velvet black tracksuit and brews kombucha tea. The living long to live more life. Cataract gives a quarter to a one-legged trombone player in Washington Square then takes ten bucks from his cup. My visions are escalating. The tiger and lamb make love. The snake and Eve commiserate. Adam takes another bite.

•

St. Sylvia clowns on the streets of Budapest for her supper when the prince finds her and makes her queen. From the seat of power she protects the Christians from being thrown over bridges. She walks the promenade with orchids in her hair. Her throat is slit by the descendants of Spanish Moors in the afternoon so everyone can see.

The man with horns in the West Indian parade has a message for you, says Darling.

What did he say, I ask.

He says you will only know yourself when you see your face.

What?

Physicists explode the world to bits to see what we're made of. The signs of everlasting life are all around us but I don't have the right eyes. Gods are dreaming up new stuff to baffle everyone and the snakes in the grasses smell with their tongues. I am stretching myself toward the streetlamps that fill the empty heavens. The news isn't even news anymore. People work and work and work for tiny numbers in the clouds. The ditch digging will never end and the thin, sad girls of the East Village all live in Brooklyn now. Eli, there is nowhere to preach the gospel, no gospel left to preach. No sun I can see. Nowhere left to lose my mind in peace.

I wish people still smoked cigarettes, you say, Eli.

They do.

Yeah. But not like they used to.

•

Below the sports bar is a grave where the dead Indians slumber. Darling and I fight all morning. She is suicidal and so am I. Then we make up with kisses and cups of black coffee and the stars of the night fading into day.

I want to marry you in a French country church with the baker as the witness, I say.

I want to marry you in the wheat field where van Gogh killed himself, she says.

Cataract is fishing in the Hudson River. He smiles at the bankers and fools, his dark eyes seeing everything but the physical world. He knows every dream we have and every fear and every highway happiness. Nono cleans the fish and they feast. They seek the carnivals and fairs and go antiquing in the good part of Bushwick. Darling's father's father was a great crooner of love songs and her mother's father owned a condom company. She darns my socks and makes my breakfast. Eli, we are men by desperate means. I rub my wings and pepper the night with prayers to my lovers and friends. I go to the chapel and weep for better ways to make my bed.

Thinking now, Eli, of all the people I have known who I don't know anymore.

I'm making a Dr. Pepper and whiskey, you say.

Make me one, too.

Perhaps we should situate ourselves in the long expanding mendacity of time. The space between the spaces between the spaces. Eli, might we come to some battle with Cataract? A final end of endings? Much of my day is spent finding something to do with my day. I'm tired. I came here for adventure and ended up with the same old restlessness and desire. I fold up my wings and walk uptown. The saints are born and live and die forever. Sick and blue, I head for the great cock of the city to fly.

You don't have to go, says Darling.

You know I do.

Go then, she says. But think of me when you fall.

I'll think of you when I fly.

It is midnight but could be morning. Eli, I've wrung my hands a good bit and gazed at my navel far too long. Up there in the clouds I will see the enemy and raise him one.

Do you really need to do this, you ask. Couldn't you just rent a helicopter?

There are many things I could and couldn't do, I say.

You know how this story ends.

No one knows how the story ends, I say. Just where they left off reading.

St. Kirk is hung from a lamppost in the waning hours of Palm Sunday as church bells toll the wrong hour. His feet are tied together with barbed wire and his eyes are pecked at by sick crows. His Hawaiian shirt is torn half off. His mother washes the blood from his feet with warm milk.

I take to the sky with my improvised wings. I am above the buildings and the parks full of dying leaves, van Gogh yellows and Gauguin reds. Listen here, Eli. I've got nothing on my mind as I mix things up from one thousand feet. My heart is an avalanche of possible things. I see Cataract driving in the sunlight laughing. I see the grey girl and the white waves lapping at her feet. The Holy Ghost sits on her face and takes the Freedom Tower in her mouth.

Might you come down a moment, you say, Eli. You have a child forthcoming.

I'm awakened from my flight.

You are a sweet man, says Darling. Her dark eyes are full of the promise of the world to never end.

Agape, agape, she says. The greatest of these is love.

I fall into the East River and no one bats an eye.

An envelope with my name left by the door. In it a square of black paper. It is winter, strange.

Darling and I walk through the nightly confusion, the red buildings and blue windows. Throngs of literate people in this city, even the man picking up cans reads Dostoevsky. In the skylights of million-dollar townhouses you can see the planes crossing above you like there is no ceiling. When you're rich, things are easy and the food is better but your soul is rotten. Serve only one master, says Christ. Eye of a needle, all that. But then again—take off your clothes, Eli, and feel how nice these high thread count sheets feel in this strangely unguarded townhouse.

•

We are maddening in the neighborhood. A film crew on the street, a show about spoiled children. Eli, you go over and scream until they give us a hundred bucks to go away.

I have a vision of Cataract and Nono at a local greengrocers in some hippie Carolina village.

Get in the car, says Cataract to Nono.

I need kale twice a day or my bowels get funky, she says.

There's no time for kale, says Cataract. Bounty's worth at least six fucking figures.

You don't have to curse, says Nono.

Cataract licks his finger to test the direction of the wind.

Yes I do, he says.

Darling and I snuggle in the January snow. We've rigged up camouflage around our bed, nicely hidden—bunnies in a briar patch. There comes forth a vision. Cataract exits his '87 Oldsmobile wood-paneled van and scopes the city. He breathes his smoke on me. I wake to a single blade of lightning.

Two old ladies smoke long cigarettes and sing the "Battle Hymn of the Republic" on the F train. Hasidic families with Hasidic babies pray to the Hasidic god. A homeless girl kicks a drink machine. Somewhere in the Middle East a war just started over a bottle rocket and a wink to the wrong girl. My mind is full of past.

•

We wake up early in the East Village, where all the good poets died. We go to our boat parked on Fourteenth. Eli, I will grab us bagels. A few coffees, black. Darling and I read the Sunday paper and relax. We are aboard our vessel minding the business that is rightfully ours. I am very much high on narcotics when this woman calls to us. A parking cop. A cartoon of a woman.

This ya boat, she says.

Lovely Rita meter maid, I say.

This ya boat, asshole, she says.

Yes, Rita. I am her captain, yes, I say.

You gotta a license? I'm gonna run these plates.

Ten minutes and cops have surrounded the boat. We are hunkered in the hull.

The fuck do we do now, Darling says.

Gimme your phone, I say.

We're gonna die, says Doubting Eli.

I just sent Hal and Al Malchow a message, I say. They got the Internet to order one thousand pizzas to this address.

Cops are too busy asking who ordered anchovies to see us backing up the boat, unhitching in the water. We're pushing off into the Hudson River. News choppers like vultures in the sky. One spotlights us. Our hair going wildly in the wind, we raise sails.

Fire two flares, Eli, I say. Distract the pilot.

Darling, I say. Grab the scuba gear.

The city behind us erupts in gunfire.

Two flares. That way, Eli.

We've found ourselves caught between a gunfight and New Jersey.

I take a hard left and we hug the coast. There is quiet out on the water as we see the statue for the first time. So lonely beside the furious city. Tough as a woman, soft as a girl.

We drop anchor and put on our scuba gear. I fall backward into the water and blow my boat a kiss goodbye. A ship so sweet she did not need a name. I hit the detonator and she explodes.

Falling to shore my mind's made up—love is an unwise and beautiful adventure. Battery Park and we've beaten back the pigs. We're presumed dead. From where we are we have a straight level shot of Lady Liberty in front of us. The Freedom Tower at our back.

Eli, you are first shift lookout tonight. If the cops come, keep them occupied with tales of lunar phenomena.

Take your hand off the wheel of time slowly. We could be happy as children running naked in their first rain. I fill Darling full of love. Her dark eyes look to heaven as if in prayer.

•

St. Oscar is assassinated while he raises the chalice at the end of the Eucharist. The altar boys think it's a firecracker lit off by one of the school bullies and continue their duties.

The snow is now coming in sideways. The broken spokes of the wheel keep spinning. A cup of black coffee and the dead famous actor with a needle in his arm. An indecent landscape out there. Not a proper backyard for miles. Down on our knees, Eli, for some heroic sign. A clue to help us clean away what's the matter.

Strange Spanish whispers from the garbage men. We are broken again. Suffering for food. Unflappable gauchos, Eli, yet Cataract is closing in.

We are tourists on this earth. We get brief access to the fire and ice. There is another message. On a menu at the little French bistro we can't afford.

I am with Nono, it reads. We're coming for you. Let's play a Manhattan-size game of chess. Black or white?

The child pains increase inside Darling. I am filled to the brim with love for our forthcoming family. History is unfolding under our feet. Chasing us. A new Christ for Yankees and Rebels.

We've got to mount a worthy defense, Eli.

Are we going to have to get the crew back together, I say.

I'm afraid so.

The Holy Ghost rises from bed and brushes her hair. The light of heaven is heavy in her eyes. She is all the women I have ever loved. She is my Darling, too. There is hunger in the bellies of babes in the arms of refugees. There is sand in my toes from the beaches of Babylon.

The planes look like they're floating, says Eli, but they are moving with incredible speed.

I tell the skywriter to spell out, WE'LL PLAY THE BLACK PIECES. YOUR MOVE.

Nono plays his queen, Darling is ours. Tuesday and Finger are rooks. Al and Hal are black knights. We are playing a human-sized game of chess throughout this island. We pay the local weirdos to be pawns.

The Aztecs believe St. Thomas is their God. I shrug at the coming apocalypse, he says.

12

e4 e5

At dawn they send a Haitian man in a dashiki to Central Park and we counter with a girl in cornrows to greet him. They are young and understand only their hormones. Our first pawns into battle.

What's Cataract doing here, Eli. Walk me through it.

Control the center.

The seasons are spiraling. The calendar pages are flying away.

What's the plan?

We wait, you say. It's his move.

f4 exf4

He moves a pawn, a crust punk, to Lincoln Square. We capture, make him make our beds. My teeth are falling out. I lose control. I can't find a bathroom. I have just learned to fly and I am falling falling falling and never hit the ground.

Wake up, says Eli.

I was never asleep.

Bc4 Qh4+

They send a Texas runaway to Murray Hill.

We have to send Darling to Hell's Kitchen, you say, Eli.

Unsafe, I say.

Darling is dog-tired on the bench and her cheeks are pink with cold. There is a brutal innocence to her. She's a pugilist against signs and shadows.

I am not weeks, she says. I am days away.

I love you, I say. I love you till dust.

I hail a cab and put my whole world inside it. Pat the trunk twice as it drives away. She smiles through the window, her eyes are a pale pale blue.

Kf1 b5

Cataract shifts himself over a block in Harlem. We put an Oxy addict up to block the crust punk in Murray Hill. My mind is of a mind to mind you, Eli. There are fighters in the streets of eerie cities tonight. Spacemen look down on earth. I am amazed by constant human error, the drop of blood spilled on the map to redemption. The deafening death rattle of those dying alone.

We're playing for our lives here, you say, Eli.

No mercy, I say.

Bxb5 Nf6

The crust punk takes our runaway and ravages her sexually in Gramercy Park. I dispatch Al Malchow to the West Village. A sun-shower looms. The devil beats his wife. A fox's wedding. Naked rain. A witch brushes her hair. Orphan's tears.

Nf3 Qh6

Cataract sends a Cuban drug dealer to threaten my Darling.

I will destroy the boy, I say.

Calm down, you say, Eli. They'll capture you.

She retreats. Her eyes, throughout the earth—they run to and fro.

We're running out of time, I say. I feel the new Lord crying out.

d3 Nh5

Cataract brings another Harlem girl on the sly to the Upper East Side. I dispatch Al to Hell's Kitchen. The winds of favor and grace. A couple cries at Papa John's. There is an accident, child and car. A dog births puppies in the gutter and the man who sells lemons dries his eyes. A girl in a jean jacket smokes and cries. The wind has started blowing at our backs.

Nh4 Qg5

A heroin addict ex-model to Hell's Kitchen. Her hair in tangles. Her lipstick all wrong.

Send Darling our Queen to threaten them, says you, Eli.

Why must we always use her as bait, I say.

You got a better idea, amateur?

Do it, I say.

Nf5 c6

Cataract moves the runaway down to the Garment District. We dispatch a hustler to block the crust punk in Gramercy.

He's bringing the fight to us, you say, Eli.

I wait beside the fading bus stop.

Coke for a smoke, says a man in dark clothes.

I keep to the downers, I say.

I got those, too.

He loads me up and I spiral down and return baptized on the side of Judas.

But he betrayed your Lord, you say, Eli. Thirty pieces of silver and a kiss.

Without him nothing happens, I say. We remain unforgiven.

The Holy Ghost blows me on the sun.

1g4 Nf6

A juvenile delinquent to Midtown. Al Malchow retreats. Millions of humans small talk through their day. I'm in the corner watching the paralyzed man roll through the street with his family. Boom and all the dead. He was a soldier once in a war against the domino effect. I remember his tattoo. A naked lady on his chest he made dance when he flexed pecs. Molly, your sister, is here with us, Eli. Her face covered in freckles, cutting herself and posing nude for the man in a three-piece suit.

Rg1 cxb5

A runaway to Morningside Heights and we take the crust punk. The air feels like Amsterdam, where they play chess with all white pieces. Bike weather with Mercury in retrograde. In the ocean somewhere baby tiger sharks cannibalize their siblings in the womb. I ache for God, Eli. Simply put.

h4 Qg6

He sends a tenderfoot to Times Square and Darling moves back to Tribeca. Darling my comfort, my home. Her hair is shaggy in a seventies way. She wears a summer dress and a leather jacket, reads a worn copy of *Light in August*. Blows me a kiss. The dying sun is so often the color of blood. We would drink milkshakes if we were not at war.

h5 Qg5

A blind Rastafarian threatens Darling, we move her away quickly.

Eli, the children's hospital is on fire.

Keep focus, you say.

A girl with golden flowers is going cross-eyed.

Cataract smells blood, he knows my child is about to arrive.

Blessed are the meek, says Eli. No mercy.

Qf3 Ng8

Nono moves to Midtown. Al Halchow retreats. There is a siren constant in the distance. Always some emergency in Manhattan. The hipsters sip gourmet whiskey out in Brooklyn. Let them live their ironic lives in peace. Sunny day. Man plays trumpet in the park. A drunk kid dry heaves. His dog nuzzles his arm.

Bxf4 Qf6

A runaway from Ohio comes crashing down to Hell's Kitchen and captures the Haitian. He threatens my Darling.

Retreat, I call to her. Come close to me.

No mercy, she says. There's no such thing.

Nc3 Bc5

A white Rastafarian to the Upper East Side and I send Finger to the East Village. He is strong now with his money and child, a tough son with his mother's eyes. Tuesday is everywhere. She's always on time.

Nd5 Qxb2

A kid named Choker goes to Union Square. Darling to Harlem.

Are we winners or losers, Eli?

Pointless question, you say.

Do you see five moves ahead?

Yes.

And do we win?

Pointless question.

I get high alone. The sky is a boring blue.

Bd6 Qxa1+

They move a bipolar girl in overalls to Little Italy. Darling takes a runaway and Cataract's in check. I see flashes of Mississippi. Long afternoons with Wise Jane and Willie. It can be strawberries and weed and daisies. I've got a good girl with her heart in the fight. No time for nostalgia. The jig is almost up.

Ke2 Bxg1

Cataract moves to lower Harlem and I send Finger to capture the ex-model in Morningside Heights.

My mind is on autopilot. The moon, Eli. Remember. The tides?

Dark matter, you say. Antimatter. Visible matter.

Who says?

They.

We're all the they there is now.

e5 Na6

Cataract moves up a break-dancer to Soho and I call Hal Malchow to the Lower East Side. I've got a head full of flowers but I am sane. I scale a co-op. It is nice, the warm night, seasons grinding out. Good night to the rich and poor. Social justice is absurd compared to the universe. We are battle ready. The end is nigh.

Nxg7+ Kd8

A Knight puts us in check. You move over to Chinatown.

I know this game, you say, Eli. He's already won.

Qf6+ Nxf6

Nono moves to Soho. A blunder. Tuesday captures her.

Be7#

Checkmate.

13

Cataract paces in the jail hallway. He smells of sage and masturbation. Some silver light enters through the window and the jailer whistles "2 Legit 2 Quit." Tuesday and Finger make out. Al and Hal play thumb war. Eli, you let Darling sleep on your shoulder.

I have a vision of losing battles fought only in dimensions and time. We were two soldiers, Eli, but now we are prisoners of war. The killers and victims unite in forgiveness. The heavens and the earth cleft from each other. We are all truly made from the same stuff. Ashes to ashes. Dust to dust.

Jailer, I call. She's going into labor. Jailer rolls his toothpick.
    Bullshit, he says.
    Her water's broken, see for yourself.
    When he opens the cell door and comes to her I hit him over the head and take his gun. Another guard sees us and Finger slams him. Al and Hal take out another.

Snowball will be here in five, I say. Just like we planned it.

I have to find Nono, you say.

There's no time, I say.

I'm going into labor, says Darling.

You don't have to pretend anymore, I say.

I'm not, she says.

I touch her belly.

I'm going to find Nono, you say, Eli.

See you on the roof, I say. The helicopter's waiting.

Maloney, Darling says. It's happening.

We run through the maze of halls. A rookie stops us and raises his gun.

Get out of here, kid, I say. I'll spare you.

The rookie gets off two shots and I pop one in his leg. We're up the stairs and more cops are close behind. I can hear the helicopter blades from the roof. I feel a sting on my back and I fall.

Maloney, you say, Eli. You're hit.

Where have you been?

I found Nono. She's on her way.

Help me up, I say and we run out the door. The helicopter is in the air. Nono comes running and at the last moment grabs your hand.

Can you forgive me, I say to Nono.

Namaste, she says.

Cataract comes out shooting blindly and the SWAT team's close behind. We head up and out over the water into the black night.

●

They call out a chopper of their own. Snowball maneuvers best he can.

I've got to put her down, he says.

Get us to the Statue of Liberty, I say.

We won't make it, he says. Not all of us.

We're going down fast. I see the statue from the corner of my eye. We get on the rope to go down.

Steady, I say.

The police helicopter is landing on the other side of the island. The whole SWAT team runs out, guns firing.

I slip and fall out into the darkness.

When I come to, I'm on your back, Eli, and you're carrying Darling in your arms up the statue stairs. The cops are close behind.

I can't wait any longer, Darling says.

We climb and climb, the thunder of boots behind us.

St. Darling's blood fills the floor of Lady Liberty's crown. A full moon is peeking in. Her eyes close as our daughter's first cries echo into the night.

I love you deep as an ocean, I say.

At Wise Jane's we are all around the warm table. Finger and Tuesday, Al and Hal, you and Nono, Darling and I. Willie dog is at our feet. There is corn and fresh tomatoes. Wise Jane passes the wine. Boom and White Mike Johnny play dead man's chess. John Lennon and Elvis are warming up in the lounge. We go to the cotton field and pass the moonshine and howl. There are birds everywhere. Birds of sapphire, birds the color of wild sunflowers. Sophia is born on a Sunday, a star that burns forever in the sky.

ABOUT THE AUTHOR

Michael Bible is originally from North Carolina. His work has appeared in *Oxford American*, *The Paris Review Daily*, *Al Jazeera America*, *ESPN: The Magazine*, and *New York Tyrant*.